THE VOYAGES OF GAEA

BY KEVIN SHOEMAKER

THE VOYAGES OF GAEA

Copyright © 2010 by Kevin Shoemaker

This book is printed on acid free paper

A Shoemaker Labs Book
Lafayette, Colorado

e-mail: Thevoyagesofgaea@gmail.com

ISBN 978-0-9815092-3-5
ISBN 0-9815022-3-1

Registered with the Library of Congress

Grateful acknowledgement is made to those who have given permission for the use of previously copyrighted material in this book. Every reasonable care has been taken to correctly acknowledge copyright ownership. The author and publisher would welcome information that will enable them to rectify any errors or omissions in succeeding printings.

Cover Art courtesy of NASA
Chapter Artwork courtesy of NASA, the Shoemaker family and Wikopedia

First edition September, 2010

Printed in the United States of America

To Judi, Leah and Stephen
for their inspiration and support

Acknowledgment

I would like to sincerely like to thank Hoffman Pilot Center in general and Harry LaForge, Jr. in particular for their editing and comments. Also, I would like to thank my friends Matt, Jason, Bud and Eliot for their editing and comments. Finally, I would like to thank my lovely wife Judi for her editing, encouragement and patience.

Table of Contents

Author's Preface

Why do certain things resonate with human beings? For instance, musical tones are not by any means random, 440 cycles per second represents the musical tone of A, above middle C. 430 cycles per second does not feel right, in fact, it sounds dissonant. There are other "resonances" like personal relationships, eating, enjoyment of art and wondering about the meaning of life. Plants and animals seem to find good places to thrive. Science Fiction is an interesting example of a resonance as well and has been with us since the inception of technology. Many people look toward the future, mostly in anticipation of new explorations, advances in medicine and new capabilities. Inherent in Science Fiction writing is technology which is one of the components a science fiction writer uses in conjunction with his or her imagination. In many cases the creative outcome has important consequences for our future. For instance, the first person to think of a rocket was a science fiction writer, so too the jet pack and International Space Station. What is this resonance?

Since the early 1900's, there have been two fundamental points of view on how the mind works. Freud, Adler, Jung and many others even today describe the workings of the mind in terms of relationships, abstractions and projections. This knowledge base has enabled many psychoanalysts, psychologists, and psychiatrists to successfully heal the mentally awry. Through their work, significant inroads into the understanding of the mind have been achieved using concepts and precepts that in many cases have deep philosophic origins. This group has been, with some accuracy, defined as the behaviorists. These researchers and therapists do not define the mind as a series of electrical stimulations or chemical operations. To them, the deepest understanding comes from the words and actions of human beings. From these words and actions, life takes place; like learning, which many define as a change in behavior based on experience.

There is another group, sometimes referred to as the behavioralists, believe that the mind, in fact, can be best understood as the propagation of electrical impulses and the exchange of chemical energies. They rely on a significant amount of scientific research, including the tracing of electrical nerve activity and the locating of areas of the brain responsible for various activities, including creativity, sensory cognition and mood manifestation. These researchers have had significant success in understanding and pin-pointing the interaction of chemicals and nerve impulses and as a result have created wonder drugs that have stemmed the tide of schizophrenia and other mental disorders. Millions have been helped from their work and can enjoy productive lives with these new understandings.

There is however, important knowledge from both

groups that the best therapists employ to fully understand the workings of the mind. And, within the recesses of the human spirit, be it conceptual or defined by some coordinate base, fundamental tenets of thought and understanding have had their origins. One of the basic tenets is the creation of science fiction. There are those gifted people who can create music or poetry or see into the future. Why we, as sentient beings, have been awarded these attributes, no one has been able so say....yet. But one thing is indisputable, there are many people who can take our current state of scientific knowledge and project it into the future. In so many cases, writers once thought of as day dreamers like Jules Verne, H. G. Wells, Arthur C. Clark, Philip Dick, Isaac Asimov, Ray Bradbury, Gene Roddenbury, ... and so many others have had accurate visions of the future. One might argue that they, in their books, influence the future. In reality their actions might best be described as prophetic. Knowledge plus creativity can lead to new vistas in thought and as a result, the door into the future is cracked just a bit to allow us to look into tomorrow.

There are those who believe that in the future, science and philosophy will become one, as by the way they once were during their inception in ancient Greece, this will probably become true once again. I wonder if at that time at the end of the halls of NASA and the European Space Agency there will be a science fiction writer, whose employers will be dependent on his or her musings.

This is our susceptance, where the waters of human essence flow into the realm of the future, pulling us into those areas illuminated by self-actualization. We have no choice, it is our destiny.

This book is a nod to those behind the pen, whose writings have guided us and opened the door to a bountiful and awe inspiring future.

K. Shoemaker
Boulder, Colorado, 2010

Introduction

It was the natural order of things. Newton and Einstein had been right, you cannot get more reaction out of action and you cannot go faster than the speed of light. The scientists had therefore determined that the only way to go to the stars was to create a very large spaceship, inhabit it with at least 1,000 people and fly for at least a few generations to visit and catalog the local neighborhood of stars, of which there are at least 510 "G" type stars, just like our own.

The "Terranauts" would be from all walks of life, screened only for skills, stable psychological demeanors and general health. They would take care of the great ship, named *Gaea* (Mother Earth, in Greek). All necessary items would be manufactured or re-cycled from used materials on the ship. All life essential things would be re-cycled like water and air. Food would come from vast greenhouses, engineered food substances and the extraction of vital nutrients from waste material.

During their voyage, constant (or at least frequent) communications would be kept with those on Mother Earth. The great radio telescopes on Earth would be tasked with maintaining a link between the "Flight Control" websites and the spaceship. Video links would be used for as long as practical, followed by lower data rate links and finally by very low data links as the craft flew amongst the stars so far away.

During the voyage, *Gaea* would gather in raw materials like Hydrogen and star dust particles which could be useful for manufacturing fuel and building materials. During the transition out of the solar system, scout craft would fly to asteroids, Apollo objects, moons, comets and other space detritus to explore and gather more useful raw materials. The universe was hoped to be, and found to be, full of these raw materials during their voyage.

There were a few fundamental rules on board the spacecraft during their flight with regards to living and working on the ship. In fact, a constitution had been carefully written up for the travelers to abide by, which was based on common sense requirements for the safe passage of the explorers. For instance, a child could not be conceived unless someone else had passed away, there was a need for a constant population based on food, living space and duties. Criminal activity was dealt with by isolating the individual in more and more mundane jobs, based on the severity of the crime. If a person was deemed to be psychotic, several types of therapy including drugs were used to control the behavior. As one could imagined, a few people were deemed "un-useful" for various reasons and relegated to the compound colloquially known as the place for "space sickness." As in regular Earth society, there were always those who needed special attention and care, this is true for almost any large group of isolated people, whether they are on an island or in space.

The size of *Gaea* was enormous and took a world wide effort to build. Much like the pyramids taking 30 to 50 years to complete, the spaceship also took a huge amount of time to assemble. The core structure spent 24 years in space before it moved under its own power. In that time, several generations of upgrades had been implemented, crowds of engineers, architects and technicians spent years aboard before launch. It was in essence a space hotel during this phase, bringing tourists as well as workers. The craft turned out to be several miles long and several miles in girth, creating thousands of sealable cavities that could withstand the rigors of space travel. Powered by solar, fusion, fission, fuel cell and hydrogen power plants, all modes of power generation were redundant and all byproducts of in-efficient power generation were used in some manner. In all, 40 power sources were used, many with 100+ years of useful power generation capabilities. The craft was highly insulated, except where the greenhouses were placed, they for the early part of the journey, generated more heat from in incident sunlight, than they used. Later during the flight, the domes where sealed to keep in the warmth and lights were used to grow the crops. These domes where complete ecosystems in themselves, much like the Biosphere 2 in Arizona, only on a much larger scale. These domes provided food and vacation venues for the crew. An incarnation of Arcosanti, this ship created the fully closed cycle life vessel imagined so long ago by Paulo Soleri.

The ship was shaped like a cylinder, which rotated to simulate gravity. Those pieces of equipment that needed to track steady objects, like the sun, were de-spun to allow steady following. The cockpit or more realistically the cockpit room, was also de-spun necessitating the absence of gravity. Flight crews had to adapt to this condition for up to 8 hours a day as they navigated, plotted and flew the great ship. At the rear of the cockpit room and in the center was a circular hallway with led to two sets of stairs radiating outward. As the crewmembers started down these stairs towards the living quarters of the ship, their weight increased step by step until they had smoothly transitioned from zero to one g. Attitude control was accomplished by Hydrogen accelerators, taking the local gases found in space and porting them through an accelerating apparatus, much like a jet engine. There where over a thousand of these devices planted over the exterior of the ship. Main propulsion was from Ion and Nuclear engines, all clustered at the aft end of the main structure. Finally there where pods of mid power engines that could be gimbaled in various direction to create enough thrust to quickly move the ship in any direction, these engines could be used for emergency maneuvers also, if required.

Qualifying for a flight on the starship meant at least a year's training at essentially a Star Fleet Academy. This included classwork, medical tests, flights to the starship and a host of other activities. It was important for the Terranauts to get used to space, to their crew members and most importantly, to their commitment to leave Earth. Anyone with second thoughts would be allowed to give up their position on the craft. Insofar as there where over 100,000 applicants, finding a replacement was not an issue. In the last months before launch, work was frenzied and the crew grew together in anticipation of the great voyage. Those on Earth related to a crew member held parties and dinners to say goodbye to their kin. It was a mixture of sadness and being proud that fell over these final family meetings.

Weeks before launch, the crew members started to move into their new world; all had visited it beforehand, but now there was no looking back. Stores and fuels were topped off, enough to make it to the "decision point," that area in space during the voyage where they could either turn back if there had been problems or go beyond if they felt they could complete the mission. Considering the speed that was anticipated during the voyage this point would come at 10 years after launch, or anytime before. Assuming that the voyage was continued towards stellar exploration, it was just possible for the very youngest crew members to get to several star systems and return to Earth, albeit at a very old age. This was determined to be the "range" of the spacecraft. Beyond that point, only strangers would return, without any direct experience with Earth or its inhabitants. It was considered the range as well as the ultimate duration of the mission. Depending on luck, interest and speed, at least five star systems could be explored and cataloged. It turned out to be many more, as the terranauts learned about more civilizations from the inhabitants of the worlds they discovered and as a consequence, were able to visit over 20 star systems before returning home.

During the initial phases of construction the retired Space Shuttles were revamped by making them into robot vessels designed to transfer large amounts of cargo to the new spaceship taking shape in orbit. The shuttles were essentially gutted, removing all life sustaining equipment. This gave the shuttle 50,000 more pounds of payload capability and thus made it a perfect vehicle to start the *Gaea* project.

Technology allowed the voyage to take place, insofar as the ship was mostly built by robots, who when reprogrammed, maintained the integrity of the vessel during the voyage. Inside, and like most complex creations of humans, there was the echoing of the human body complete with nerve center, motion control, conduits of necessary nutrients and centralized, specialized areas for maintaining the health of the "organism." It was in many ways a projection of humanity and could have been humanoid in appearance if that wasn't so inefficient for space travel. Technology created the nerve center or central command post, where navigation and ultimate ship commands were sent from. Banks of computers and electronics enabled communications between all crew members and communications with those on Earth. Some memory banks held the complete written works of humanity and others recorded every moment of the voyage. Much of this new information was sent back to Earth but as the ship became more distance, lower data rates were required, necessitating decisions on importance.

There were hierarchies of computational requirements. The first and foremost layer was that of several supercomputers that redundantly monitored ship's health and activities. The next layer was more in the laptop range where the computational power was good enough to enable scientists and engineers to do their work. The lowest layer was that of the programmable arrays. These devices could be made to be any analog or digital component with billions of "gates", allowing all simpler functions to be carried out. These devices could be reprogrammed if necessary to create different functions. All layers could communicate amongst themselves.

The launch was a worldwide event, anticipated for years and watched by most left on Earth. With the crew aboard, a thousand channels active, and politicos on earth looking for air time, the commander of the ship gave the order to launch. As the Ion propulsion started to push the ship slowly, excitement increased on the ground. The ion engines had very little thrust, but output velocities near the speed of light. It in fact took the ship several days at full thrust, to leave Earth's gravitational influence. Within a week the velocity exceeded 50,000 miles per hour and within a year the velocity was over 70,000 miles per second. Halfway to the first star system, the ship had to be reversed in orientation and thrust applied for the slow de-acceleration.

Once beyond Earth's gravitational influence, *Gaea* flew to Mars and then Jupiter to increase its velocity using the slingshot effect that was employed by so many inter planetary satellites. To keep fully supplied and to cover unexpected problems, supply rockets were sent out from Earth using a mass produced high acceleration launch vehicle. Normally these vehicles were launched with a frequency of about one per month. More if there was an emergency. Due to the increasing speed of the main ship, these supply ships showed up at different times to dock with the main ship. In this way, the crew was fully covered in terms of material needs during its initial part of the long voyage.

During the multi-year voyage, enormous change took place. Essentially unanticipated events shaped the lives of the crew members. Mostly for the better and some events due to the rigors of space travel. Primarily, the crew became adjusted and happy aboard the ship. The conversion came quickly, within months as the crew members found new friends, activities and jobs. Friends grew into social pods, where people of like interests spent time together. Social similarities attracted them, as on earth. Clubs emerged along with teams for sport and "universities" for further learning. As for activities, there were a multitude of social gathering zones, almost all sports were represented in arenas and fields. Those who wanted to run or ski made use of the circular tracks around the perimeter of the ship, over a mile in circumference, that had various environmental zones including lakes, mountains and forests. The requirement for plant life was integrated into the landscapes. Jobs were plentiful and offered pathways to upper echelons based on experience and learning. There was a hierarchy of command structure that although not military in composition, was layered enough to represent a small government on earth. The commander had a four year term and was chosen from a pool of "chief executives" who were responsible for the safe operation of the ship. The chief executives managed areas such as propulsion, navigation, science, communications, environmental controls, social issues, medical needs and a other vital concerns. The "CEs" had staffs with layers of required personnel below. Everyone aboard had a job and responsibilities. There were workdays of approximately eight hours each. For a while the ship divided in roughly three parts, along the longitudinal axis at 120 degree intervals. This allowed people to rotate in and out of jobs over a 24 hour period, thereby covering all watches and ship's needs. After a few years however it was found that more and more people liked to be awake with others at the same time, gravitating toward a 2/3 population being awake at the same time.

The social discovery during the first several years of voyage was that the inhabitants of the great ship found themselves at ease, it felt like they had all moved to a particular island on Earth and adjusted as necessary to feel comfortable. Many crew members spoke of it being their home, good enough to be born, live and die in. Not to say that there weren't any problems on board with personal conflicts and other issues, it was just that the ship was so large that no one wanted to "go outside." It was the natural order of things.

The journey to the first compelling planet took many years to accomplish. The last year at full speed allowed the crew members to get close enough to view the first world with possible life through the telescopes and sensor arrays. The fourth planet of this solar system had an atmosphere, water, and evidence of life via the trace elements in the atmosphere. The astronomers picked it out as a very likely prospect for observation and visiting. It looked safe, had no radio emissions and at best, a pre-industrial society. Methane indicated the possible presence of animals and possibly humanoids. Several months before closest approach, they were still in reverse thrust and about one million miles away. The idea was to scan the planet as best they could, decide if they wanted to go into orbit by slowing further or continue on a hyperbolic trajectory onto the next planet that looked promising. At this distance, significant detail could be viewed of the surface, weather patterns and atmospheric composition. Because the ship was a dark color, the possible inhabitants of this world would not be able to see them until their closest approach and only if they had the proper telescopic equipment. The astronomers started to see details of animal and humanoid activity including lights and telegraph like operations. They found that the planet had an ocean, although it was only half of the planet's composition. It appeared that there was nautical activity with ships and possibly railways or roads on the surfaces of the various "continents." Somethings remain the same about life in the universe. First, existence through hunting and foraging, then life advances into an agrarian state, then societies claim the land and finally the global morass adjusts and looks to the stars for answers.

Those who liked to write were asked to report, document and comment on the new worlds and their inhabitants. Some of these stories were radioed back to Earth, most were stored for further review and analysis. Videos, holograms, and still pictures were also created to complete the documentation. In several cases, sentient extra-solar inhabitants came back as explorers, hopefully to complete *their* trip on a second voyage of the starship.

The chronicling of the discoveries of *Gaea* are told in the following pages. What was anticipated rarely happened. What was amazing occurred frequently. Thirty eight of the original crew members returned to earth, accompanied by 952 homo sapiens and 130 other life forms from various planets. Many original crew members stayed on the newly discovered worlds. The cultures the Terrans discovered were both new to them and in a way, familiar. It came as a shock to find that the problems Earth had dealt with were issues on other planets as well. The inhabitants might not look the same, rarely as it turned out, but the societies created on these planets where, as on Earth, necessary for survival. The data banks upon the return of *Gaea* had some technological descriptions of newly discovered apparatuses but mostly had stories of life on other planets, about the same ratio as in Earth's data banks.

APHRODITE 4

"Every adult needs a child to teach; it's the way adults learn."
- Frank Clark

By Judee Dublin, chronicler and teacher

Day 1

Breathtaking. The first planet to be examined in detail shines in the night. Shines from reflections of its two small moons glinting off of its nighttime side. Shines inside the souls of crew members years in their travels to find other worlds. The ocean is blue, even from a great distance. This planet is almost as beautiful as our own. The crew members of our ship monitor the visual and scientific channels during their work shifts and especially during their off periods. Almost all of the monitors are tuned in to it, with commentary from the scientists. It looks wonderful, especially after this long trip. We have been viewing it in great detail for several months now and we have been advised that large meetings will take place soon with the operational staff to discuss our intentions when we go into orbit. The decision was made a few weeks ago to enter orbit, as it looked like the inhabitants of this world did not have the wherewithal to send rockets or other destructive things at us to do us harm.

When this world was first considered for

2

exploration, most of us talked about how to handle the encounter with the life on the surface, assuming we would take out the landers and fly down there to visit personally. The staff had advised us that if we go, only a few select people would visit initially, scientists mostly and a commander. They would gather information as quickly as possible and return to the ship. If the feeling amongst that crew was that there was little or no danger for another landing, that would be accomplished with a longer stay. After that, committees would decide if some of us could go down as well. I want to go, for sure. I am an early childhood specialist and if there are societies down there, our team will need my expertise to chronicle the early educational process of their society.

Day 2

I got off work today, tired but excited about this trip. I am really happy here and now have the opportunity to experience something amazing. Back to my room now to check the main channels for new information and to prepare for a possible visit. I am on the short list, one of the first 100 to be qualified for the trip. Time for getting all of the appropriate information and plan to attend the meetings to decide on a possible introduction to the inhabitants below. Here is what we know so far:

There are advanced activities going on with regard to farming, mobility and communications.

It appears they have the equivalent of cities.

They are carbon based, in terms of life and the creation of energy. They burn campfires, burn coal (or something very much like it) and have a smattering of various reasonably complicated chemicals in their atmosphere indicating more than alchemy and less than synthesis.

Groups collect together outside of the cities on a periodic basis for some unknown function (or functions). We see monuments and special buildings for this purpose.

There are reasonably large explosions every once in a while in certain locals, not sure what this means but we will not go to those places initially.

On the night time side of the planet (it spins every 30 hours) there appears to be low levels of lighting across the population centers from an unknown source.

There appears to be no nuclear activity going on.

There appears to be no aviation.

From this information we can deduce many things. One has to be careful though not to assume that the

4

experiences of Earthlings will be germane to extra-solar planetary exploration. My primary job as I see it, is to be an active observer. I can't take my books of Piaget or Vgotsky's theories of learning down there as I can't assume their brains develop and function as ours and I would be little more than a missionary with an agenda. We cannot under any circumstances, pollute this world. That will be near impossible, just our presence will be in their stories and myths for their future. What would be interesting however is if the more fundamental activities are similar to those described by anthropologists on Earth. The fundamental precepts and mores of any of our societies could be in some way universal. I cannot wait to see these activities myself, assuming that things work out on the initial visits.

They have just announced the first landing, to be made in a deserted area of the planet, solely for the purpose of gathering samples of their atmosphere and land. Anpaytoo, the Sioux woman on C deck commented in the hall, "so we take years to get here, then we go down to sample their air and take a bit of their land." Irony of course but I told her we probably would return the theft with gifts of our own. She gave me a sardonic look. We come in peace and bring baggage.

~The Voyages of Gaea~

Meetings tomorrow are set to discuss the details, but the initial terranauts have been selected and are getting prepared. It will happen in the next several days as we have entered orbit and might become visible to the inhabitants below. I am getting nervous about this but have to concentrate on the possible large scale visit from the first tier of explorers, me included. To bed early and finish my work quickly tomorrow to get to those meetings.

Day 3

My shift is now complete, couldn't sleep very well last night. I run down the hall for an orientation from the senior staff, invitation only. Down the green hall for 100 yards, then the blue hall to level eight. Left around the corner to the wooden doors and in. Guards (or ushers depending how you look at it) are present and send me to an assigned seat. This is getting serious. Lights dim, then the commander himself comes out to a smattering of nervous applause. He has a suit on with patches and other symbols, I'd only seen him on the monitors before, quite a sight in person.

"Good evening," he starts, "take your seats quickly please, we have a lot to go over."

6

I settle into the seat shifting nervously, pull a pen and notebook out to take down details.

"As all of you know by now we are maneuvering into a stable orbit above this new world which we are tentatively calling Aphrodite 4, sister planet to Earth, if all goes well." Some quiet laughter is heard. "We are sending a crew of four down to a semi-mountainous area tomorrow for the initial survey. If all goes well we will start to send larger and larger groups of people to try to peacefully encounter the inhabitants. Based on our observations, we have determined that the next group that could go down will be the people in this room."

I look around and find that there are only about 20 of us here. I am on the final list. This means my life is about to change.

The commander continues, "You have been selected based on your skills and expertise. You were also selected by your managers as appropriate for this mission. That means we can trust you. That means you will follow the orders of the Chief Executive that will command your team. There will be no deviation from any orders allowed as this first set of encounters will be critical. Anybody with independent thoughts will be escorted back to the landing craft and zip tied to a rail. No exception, as I said before, this mission is critical. We have to leave the impression that we mean no harm and would like to do no more than to learn from these 'people.' Your present assignments have been suspended and you all will report tomorrow morning to A deck, terranaut quarters. Your lives are about to change."

With that the commander pushes a button on his lectern to bring the lights back up and exits right through a door off of the stage, briskly.

I sit there a bit stunned, wondering what an educational consultant is going to be tasked with. Why did the priority for my job become so important?

I walk back to my cabin and try to calm down and get ready for my change in occupation. Check the monitors for any last piece of information, check my e-mails for any other clues from my friends or work mates, just the standard stuff greets me. I crawl into bed and try to view some inane variety show to lull me to sleep. For some time I drift off and get some good rest, then at 3:00 AM or thereabouts, I wake up startled.

"They found children," I mutter, sitting up in bed in a dim room, lit only by the light of nearby planets and stars.

Its about the children, my life's work has been around the education of young children. The care and feeding of young minds is most important. The educational

8

approach has to be carefully thought out. Children come in a very wide variety of personalities, energy and learning styles. All must be gathered and taught, it is and will always be the way of civilized societies. We get the best out the children if they are given a wonderful venue and properly guided opportunities to question and explore the world.

They have children down there, and they need me to assess the educational process. How did they find that out?

I roll over, energy from the revelation dissipating to allow me to sleep. Eyes open for a while, half mast for a while, then silence.

Day 4

The morning comes quickly, solar shades go up on cue. I shower, dress and move into the kitchen area for some breakfast. Monitors on for the latest, nothing really being reported. I receive a call from one of my workmates.

"What is happening? They came in last night and moved your stuff...told us you are changing jobs for a while," reported my friend Sue.

"Oh, don't worry," I say, "I have to move to A deck for a while, to train for a possible mission to the surface soon. But I can't go into any details until they let me talk

9

about it further."

I go on, "They're going to send Mary Caukins down, she's wonderful."

"I know of her," Sue says, "She's magic with kids, but are you going to be okay?"

"I'll be fine and please don't worry about me, its a very exciting opportunity and I will let you know as much as I can about it. See you tonight for dinner?"

"Sure, how about Noodles?"

"Perfect, see you there at six."

I get my pack together for the day, look at my cabin, may not to see it for a long while, close the door and go down the hall, past the arboretum (which I love) to the long escalator to main spine. The gravity is a bit less here, farther from the outside. You can move faster but you have to get used to the fact that you weigh 70% of your normal weight. I go about ½ a mile to the facilities section, where air and water are produced. It rumbles with activity and smells busy. Further beyond the facilities, through the computer farms (its colder here) and finally to the command area. I have been here only on tours before, even after 10 years. I go up to a lobby area for a clearance, obtain a badge with a holographic patch and follow instructions to the A deck and terranaut quarters.

10

"A deck, level 2, room 2A, Chief Exec Osiris, 9 o'clock, seat 14," read my orders. Life was changing, no more pleasantries or informal conversations with the boss. "Osiris? Where did he get that name, isn't that the name of the Egyptian god of the dead? Great."

I walk quickly to the assigned room and to the assigned seat, open my laptop computer and look up the name out of curiosity. "God of the dead and of re-birth. Ok, its a bit better."

The Chief Exec comes in right on time, sits down at the head of the table and says "I am Chief Executive Osiris (pronounced Oh, sir, us) and will be leading this group in, if all works out, for up to three weeks on the surface of Aphrodite 4. We will train together intensively. I need to know all of you personally and you need to know me. It is imperative that you understand that we will run this like a military mission. Everyone follows orders, we get in and we get out; the amount of time might be hours to weeks, we don't know yet. The most important thing to understand is that we are there to learn, not teach. It is their planet, not ours.

11

~The Voyages of Gaea~

Day 5

The first team flies down to the surface, careful to avoid bio cross contamination, using sterile procedures and quietly observes the indigenous inhabitants. It's as if they were descendants of dinosaurs, although much smaller and walking erect. They have scales, tails and seem to be a combination of humanoids and birds. Different but not menacing. They did not experience the catastrophic meteor impact earthlings did 65 Million years ago, and this is the result. They have a full range of emotions, take care of their young, play games, farm and have homes that are reasonably sophisticated.

There is a chance meeting with the inhabitants at the end of the explorative trip. They are curious but cautious. Village leaders are called in to try to communicate with the terranauts. At first, the going is slow; common ground is found by pointing at objects and each side articulating the name. Within a few hours, a method to talk is devised. Both groups become at ease and the terranauts indicate that although they must leave, others will return to continue the visit. Gifts of a sort are exchanged, the locals give trinkets and what appear to be animistic objects. The terranauts leave objects that will not advance the local group technologically but will give the impression of worth.

12

What becomes apparent is how easily a visit from an advanced civilization can modify an indigenous culture. For instance, giving a weapon to one group can allow it to dominate all others, an artificial evolutionary step from a technological point of view. This must be avoided at all costs. The rule that comes out the first visit to another inhabited planet must be done in a sterile manner, leave nothing of consequence in either physical or intellectual form.

Day 6

The first crew returns for de-brief after which I am asked to participate in meetings with some of the terranauts. Gathered in a small room with two "originals" I listen, take notes and prepare to meet the new civilization. I am excited beyond compare but need to maintain a cool, professional vernier to accomplish the most important work of my life. I am assigned to go in the next few days and to meet with families and possibly with children. I gather my early childhood "tools" consisting of puzzles, manipulatives, materials for creative expression, art, a small musical device, and other things that will allow the children to express themselves. These objects will let the children project themselves, in other words, their feelings, their view

13

of their world.   They will teach us many things as we observe them playing with these materials.   It seems the people on the surface are open minded and eager to interact with us which should create the venue for a fruitful interaction with the children.   The objects go into a backpack, I review my notes, send some questions via the web to the just returned crew and try to get some sleep.

Morning comes quickly, the new crew musters in one of the auditoriums, loosely, not in formation.   The commander arrives and talks to us about the importance of this research.

"We cannot pollute the population, we must leave very little behind and take with us a bounty of information and impressions.   The science will be in the careful observation and interaction with this culture, the art will have to occur once we back on board *Gaea.* We need both, but remember always that we will be the stuff of legends once we leave, we are extremely impressive to them and any personal opinions or preference we emote will make its way into their culture. Ok, then, lets be careful out there and I look forward to your reports."

With that we are shepherded into outfitting rooms for special "decon" suits, no insignias, we know who the commander is and the structure of our group.   No non essential equipment, just audio and visual recorders. Me with my backpack. This is happening so quickly, I just go from meeting to dressing to mustering to eating to preparing and on and on. Within a few hours we are ready, and I do not know what to expect, but I run down the halls like everyone else, to shuttle bay number two, named Heraclitus.

We strap in with the aid of technicians, check our oxygen, check our communications and prepare for launch. After what seems to be 20 minutes, a hissing starts that indicates pressurization. It slows after a bit, then communication topics change to words like latches, deployment and umbilicals. Lights dim, the hissing stops and out of our viewports, darkness emerges as the landing bay door is opened. Its quiet now, quiet and dark...then movement, the whole ship departs its moorings like a large boat leaving dock. G forces come from an undetermined direction as we are strapped in very tightly. The darkness changes as we leave the ship, lowering our right "wing" to glide towards the planet's surface. The spherical shape of the world corrects itself to be symmetrically displayed over the front cockpit windows. The arc is obvious and we are all reminded of Earth, so far away and so long ago. In silence we glide, punctuated only by pilot talk on the comm system.

15

~The Voyages of Gaea~

I feel wonderful for a minute, this is freedom in a way, this is like gliding through the Caribbean, 20 feet below the surface, looking at amazing things, but still encased in protective clothing, just a bit isolated from the true surroundings.

The ship glides and maneuvers swan like, in an elegant suspended way, as we make our way to the surface. Then we encounter the atmosphere, we hear noise of wind rushing and observe the superheated air dancing across the front windshields. We feel buffeting, the ship reacts to keep us on course, the wings start to be effective. After many minutes of action, we are feeling slightly uncomfortable. Our limited training did not really prepare us for the true experience. The shuttle slows now, regains its composure and banks towards its destination. We relax and look forward to what is outside the main hatch. The craft banks again, nose elevates, thrusters announce the imminent landing. Then we start to brace ourselves, although the landing will be done at zero velocity, it seems like a natural reaction. The shuttle alights onto a wide open field, touches down effortlessly (thank you engineers) and the pilots follow their shutdown checklists. Voices in the background start talking about seat belt release, pressurization stabilization, quality checks. The

16

gravity feels funny, we have been living for years within a rotating barrel, where gravity comes from a concave surface, unlike the Earth and this world, which seem convex. We do not have the feeling that we are constantly walking up hill. I look into the eyes of some of the others and wonder if anyone is going to feel so comfortable that they will stay.

We move our way to the cabin doors and carefully walk down the stairway to the planet's surface. This feels a bit strange as well, but it does not take long to feel back to normal. We group up with the chief exec and take our final orders before dispersing.

"Ok, this is it, be professional, notice everything," he intones, "these are friendly people, but do not let your guard down, not so much for danger but for contamination. Learn more about them than they do of us. Report back here in four hours."

I gather with the society dynamics group and walk towards an area near a forest of very unfamiliar plants and trees to wait for the inhabitants. No doubt they have heard us land, and I saw villages through the view screens while we were descending. We find places to sit and get situated. It does not take very long for the first people to reveal themselves. Curious is the first adjective I can think of as

17

they approach, slowly but still in a determined manner. We rise, and find ourselves on average a bit taller than the inhabitants. We know we are the aliens and think about how we would react if on Earth another space borne civilization visited us. Its much the same here. They stop at about 5 meters distance and murmur amongst themselves. Our language specialist moves forward and after studying the interactions of the first visit, uses hand gestures and sounds to relax the people, pointing to various objects, then us, then back to the natives. Native only in the sense that this is their home, not in the sense of their cultural level, for we do not know anything about that yet.

The people we are looking at are as their images revealed, a combination of species that was the natural creation of millions of their years of evolution. I think now that there will never be any two planets' inhabitants that look the same. I feel sure of it because their long term histories can never be the same, their environments or even their anthropology.

Its wondrous, I feel like I want to run over and see them up close, but I cannot until they make a welcoming move. Also, this is not an emotional visit, it is one of science and observation. I wait. Within minutes however, the group moves closer, the ice is broken, we all relax a bit. There are males, females and offspring in the group. They are all curious, however the adults eyes blink more rapidly than the offspring. The offspring stay behind the females until allowed to move forward. This happens soon after the two groups converge and start to interact. My crew members all take one or two of the "Aphrodites" as we will call them and start the familiarization process. I am singled out by a family with several children and greet them. Their eyes are kind but cautious. The children slowly emerge from behind the adults and instinctively I lower myself to their level so as not to overwhelm them. The adults follow and we find ourselves all on the same eye level, they are fascinated with me and reach out to touch my arm and face. The children, as innocent as our own, move quickly to me sensing that I am no danger. This is the same in both worlds which makes me feel that I will be able to learn a great deal from them. The adults and I make conversation with the limited set of sounds we have learned from the first visit. More "words" are learned, several of mine are spoken by them. They are a very intelligent species. Soon the children find their way to my backpack and slowly I remove it, place it in the center of the circle we have formed and open it. The adults are interested in the texture and construction of the pack, the children immediately find the contents. They

19

share the objects and are soon completely engrossed by their shape and feel. The wonderment they emote is much like our own children; grasping, manipulating and exploring the various things. They find a way to fill one with dirt, like a dump truck and make noises as if they are driving down roads to drop the loads and return for more. They interact with the music machine, discovering its sounds and reacting to pleasant tones, even chords. The puzzles are a hit as well. They mimic or project their experiences in their world with these toys and soon are completely comfortable with my presence. The adults, seeing this, turn to me to find out if we have offspring; I show them a picture on the view screen of my visual recording device, they react with a sense of joy, pointing to the images and articulating words I have not heard yet as they do. They produce images, like photographs from their packs and say the same words. It is a powerful connection, I feel like I could work with them and their children with little effort.

I spend over four hours with this family, who bring in other children and other parents to show me images of their families. At the end of this period, they clearly understand that I work with children and share a special bond with them. The adults sense my expertise, admire it and sensing that my presence will not last forever, challenge me

20

to interact with one of the offspring who evidently possesses some special needs.

This child looks different than the rest, mostly in terms of his affect. The body is young but the eyes are much older. His command of the language is much closer to the adults than to the children I have met. During the hours the family and I have spent together I have learned when they are concerned about something, and they are concerned about this child. Through broken language I find out that he does not age at the same rate as others, in fact I think he ages at a rate of about 1/3 of the rate of the others. The opposite of Progeria, perhaps this child's genetic structure is such that the cells in his body replicate perfectly allowing him to appear much younger than he really is. I want to take tissue and DNA samples but that is out of the question, for now.

The adults look for answers from what they perceive as an advanced group of visitors. I think they will be disappointed to find out that we struggle with similar issues with our offspring. The only course of action is to be patient, observe, learn and take a sensitive approach to accommodating the situation. I offer an empathetic concern and communicate to the adults that their child will experience his own unique journey and not to think of him

21

as mal-formed just unique. As I prepare to leave, they look at me, then the child, hopefully with a more compassionate eye.

The chief exec calls us in to a gathering site.

"We need to return to the ship, consolidate your notes and return to the shuttle," he says.

I check my recorders, look one last time at the inhabitants, one last look at the children and return the landing site. I wonder about the special child and, taking a deep breath, hope for his success in life.

Walking back, I find myself actually looking forward to getting back "home." I wonder what is next, for me and for us as a crew. Its important that we continue exploring, its important that we continue learning.

Epilogue:

When the next exploration ship returned to the planet many years later a young adult, who had applied for passage to Earth, smiled upon entering this ship, smiled an enormously satisfied smile. This was the completion of a near lifelong dream. It took years for the applications to go from Aphrodite 4 to Earth and return, allowing his passage. This person was very special as he was the object of interest during the first visit of the Terranauts. A talented teacher had interacted with him, adjusted the educational approach of his parents and teachers and as a result, his enormous intellect was allowed to blossom. He had an unusual growth rate, as he matured at a normal mental level but grew at a much reduced physical level. As a result this young adult looked 15 but had the mind of a 40 year old. He was able to absorb all of the available written works of his world and interact with information that became available from the terranauts after a communications agreement was accepted by both planets. He was a very special person, a genius of his race. His education was not complete however, he needed to be challenged by Earth bound universities and he most of all needed to find his teacher.

COROT 7B

*"Imagination will often carry us to worlds that never were.
But without it we go nowhere."*

- Carl Sagan

~The Voyages of Gaea~

We broke orbit after a very interesting exploration of the surface of Aphrodite 4. It was a beautiful place, with wonderful inhabitants, many of whom we interacted with. The next closet star system was a year and a half away, enough time to understand the first encounter with another planet's peoples. The next encounter would be done in a more careful manner in some aspects.

The focus again would be on non-contamination. A noble if not impossible goal. Our mere presence caused contamination. But now we were wiser from our last encounter.

Life went on as normal in *Gaea,* everyone settled back into their routines, be it science or infrastructure. The change in command took place with a small ceremony, one of the chief execs was promoted, she would do well.

The next world we named CoRot 7b, as it was the 7th planet from their sun, and somewhat dark, based on our telescopic observations. As we got closer we discovered that it was in fact highly vegetated and either rotated about its axis very slowly or not at all. We surmised that life on the dark side, if in fact it did not spin, was minimal. Life on the "sunny" side on the other hand would be abundant. How would plants adapt to sun all day every day? Our computational models had a hard time predicting the plant

25

life but if anything was certain, chlorophyl would be minimal.

The day came when we, after due consideration, came into orbit and observed the world below in great detail. After several weeks further, we made the decision on a landing site, selected a small exploratory crew, and made the trip to the surface.

Again, an open area was chosen, somewhat near a village or small city. The terranauts carefully contacted the inhabitants, made their assessments and came back to the ship. Again, after due consideration, a larger landing party was selected, I was one of the lucky ones.

A specialist in sociology, I was asked to report on my (smaller) group's activities as well as my own. The focus would be on social interactions and assessing the level of cultural sophistication. The assumption was made that we were ahead of them technologically, as their communications were primitive, their level of pollution a bit high and their aviation capabilities in the formative stages.

The landing was made a few days later, with a somewhat welcoming crowd waiting for us. Morphologically, they were significantly different than us, with smaller eyes, much darker skin little body hair. On the whole they were friendly and we soon struck a common language and had an extended stay on the surface.

Quickly however, there became a serious concern as we caused a great stir with the inhabitants, when after about 18 hours, we settled into a sleep. They had not expected this and found it hard to understand. They stood around us during our sleep period and worried that we had fallen ill or simply expired.

During this period of discovery, we also found out that their way of defining time implied that they lived for a much smaller length of time than humanoids. In fact, the average life expectancy was around 30 earth years.

The conclusion of course was that this species did not sleep, and had evolved from a diurnal cycle life style like our own to a single life of awakeness. Useful in some ways we thought, but impossible for us to adapt to. As for our visit, they patiently awaited for us to come back to life after a rest. At first we stood watch to make sure they would not do anything unexpected. After several days however, it was obvious that they, although alarmed by our actions, where only curious and would not hurt us. Guards therefore were no longer necessary.

This species had adapted to their planet, essentially one side of constant sun and one of constant darkness. The sunny side defined life in significantly different terms as the dark side, which as it turns out had another species

27

which was in many ways the physical opposite of the one we were now dealing with. On the sunny side, plants had little photosynthetic actions, just constant growth without a break and they like the people, had shortened lives as a well. The constant vigilance and awareness does not let the nervous system relax, as a consequence the old story about "the candle that burns brightly, burns quickly" was true in this case. They dreamed like the Terrans, only while active, standing up so to speak. The only way one could tell a dream was in progress was to observe carefully the actions of the indigenous people, for they would slow down in their activities and sometimes stare into space for a long period of time. Dreams appeared to be necessary for both our species, necessary to make sense of our collective experiences.

The children quickly grew up in an environment filled with school in the "morning", work in the "afternoon", school at night, work until "morning", then back to the schedule again the next day. The pace was horrendous but the rate of social accomplishments was also impressive. They built, researched and lived life on a non-ending continuum of activity. Their "days" or as they call it "cycles," were about 36 hours long, with interspersed rest periods.

This of course tired the terranauts more, witnessing

the constant action and being the object of curiosity on their "off" time.

The decision was made to explore the dark side, by traveling along the equivalent of highways through the dusk (or dawn if you wish) regions towards the side of constant darkness. Using their shuttles on short jaunts the terranauts stopped after an hour of earth time as they flew towards the closest position of the terminator.

Time by the way was to a great extent irrelevant, there were no cycles to adjust to, just the constant march of activities. Instead there was a temporal reference to a particularly important event in their culture, many of our years ago. They had an especially cogent philosopher who discussed the relevance of interpreting shadows, those projected by the sun on a darkened wall of a cave for instance. The allegory was very similar to that in Plato's writings. Shadows in this culture represented the unknown, subject to speculation and subject to misinterpretation. This culture feared the darkness and embraced the light. Interestingly they had very little knowledge of the universe as a result. Their version of the cosmos came mainly from the development of radio telescopes, where they explored the actions of the sun and major radio astronomical sources. This of course led to only one particular view of

29

the universe and the knowledge that the terranauts brought down from their ship both impressed and concerned the inhabitants. It is interesting how cultures embrace their knowledge, afraid to freely explore the knowledge of others. In all cases however the more serious scientific types of people slowly make their discoveries, whether controversial or not. Whether complete or not, science marches on.

The terranauts moved towards the terminator in a methodical fashion, taking notes about the culture as they went. One thing became clear as they moved, that the cultures were influenced by their environment, especially the light levels. As they approached the area of dawn/dusk, moods and levels of activities changed. Some inhabitants in fact slept or at least rested for long periods of time. They chose darker places to do this activity. These people on a whole were less tense and could in fact relax to the point of uselessness. Moods improved markedly and although the terranauts were still a very new addition to their environment, the locals embraced them with fascination and warmth. "A proper balance" the away team leader once remarked.

Near the border they passed through a mountain range, one side lit up brilliantly at its peaks and plunged into to darkness at its base. The scene never changes and is

30

representative of the stark differences at the terminator as well as the influence of this environment on the people.

They proceeded farther into the darkness to find the dreamy realms of speculation. It became harder to find local people as they went deeper. Those they did encounter were careful and withdrew if anxious. They found travelers, those who would venture into the sunlight and return to the darkness. They found people who slept and those who discovered camp fires.

Interestingly, they found time. Many of the people of this region discovered the movement of the stars and local planets. Night was full time in the areas where their version of an astronomer was found. They understood the motion of their planet around their sun, they understood the motions of the planets and thus the periodicity inherent in celestial bodies. From this knowledge they devised calenders and clocks. They devised methods to synchronize their clocks around the terminator, depending on their "longitude." They had stories about their constellations, some of which grew into almost religious level allegories.

To them, the "sun" people were crazy and thus deserved their short lives. The "night" people on the other hand, slept relaxed and as a result had much longer lives.

It was a cultural clash of sorts, with the "mountain" people as buffer to try to understand both extremes.

Father, much farther into the dark side of the planet the terranauts ventured.   Far from the terminator, they found humanoids that had adapted to constant darkness and would never be able to venture into the light.   These beings had much larger eyes, pale if not translucent skin and an enhanced sensitivity to heat.   They hid upon the arrival of the terranauts, clustered together in fear and significant light stimulation, as the visitors had to have lights, night vision goggles and beacons to see.   The away team got as used to darkness as possible, finding the stars, milky way and planets able to provide sufficient light, but this took time. Once the away team dark adapted, the local inhabitants came out with curious unblinking eyes to examine the strange visitors. Another factor was the cold, which pervaded the surroundings, necessitating the inhabitants to live in caves and wear significant clothing. There was very little vegetation in this area, what did exist was near black in color, filled with a special photosynthetic fluid which drew energy from what few photons that existed and as a result conducted chemical reactions with the soil to derive nutrients. The indigenous plant life was edible, just barely, most of the inhabitants ate these plants and hunted for wildlife in the form of burrowing animals and cave dwelling creatures. The life was harsh and primitive, they had no time for philosophic discussions and viewed the cosmos as light giving only.

Beyond even these lands there appeared, at least from the scans of the mother ship, to be life of some sort, although very tenuous. The away team, exhausted from their journey and the cold, decided to return to the main ship, collect their recordings and write down their impressions.

From these data and from interviews with the team members, journal entries were written.

It was a spectrum of life unexpected, hot to cold, light to darkness, frantic to reserved. The report was sent back to Earth and the great ship readied for trip to the next star system.

Would they ever achieve space travel? Only the night time inhabitants understood the cosmos but lacked the technology necessary to fly, let alone rocket into space.

The cultures on CoRot 7b were so diverse based on the lack of planetary rotation, that the terranauts surmised that technological growth would be slowed as a result.

33

~The Voyages of Gaea~

L'QUACIOUS 5

"All truths are easy to understand once they are discovered; the point is to discover them."

- Galileo

On the way there, the instruments quivered and quaked causing some alarm amongst the navigational astronomers. Fields of energy probed much like radar beams, some of high intensity, some of low but with wider bandwidths. The commander listened to the concerned scientists, the energy probes were coming from the next star system, but at a significant distance.

"Is there any evidence of modulation? Is it intelligent?" the commander asked.

"We're not sure," chief scientist Cathy O. said. "There are random patterns and if we look at the spectral distribution of the energy, it cannot be a natural phenomena, there are periodicities that look designed. We have brought in a mathematician to examine the data for non random or repeating energy."

"Ok, but understand that the council and I are getting nervous about this probing, and as you know this ship takes a lot of space to reverse course. I want everyone who can contribute to this issue to be working on it, if there is any concern or sign of danger, I need to know immediately," the commander said gruffly, moving closer the chief scientist.

"I understand, we have brought on several more instruments and telescopes to aid us. We will report on a regular basis and let you know if there is any immediate danger," Dr. O. intoned, knowing full well that she would step up the analysis and would not stop until a satisfactory explanation was found.

"Regular is not good enough, I need a report every two hours, you may report by teleconference." the commander said, turning and walking away.

"Absolutely, I shall get back to you at....0200," Dr. O. reported.

"Good, thank you," was the echoing, retreating reply.

Dr. O. moved quickly down the hallway to the central cluster of laboratories dedicated to astronomical research. She walked into a conference room, motioned to several scientists to join her and sat down by the teleconference laptop. Hitting several keys, she got the immediate attention of several lab managers and other scientists.

"I need you all on line in five minutes." she said. "We have some work to perform." A multitude of voices responded, all in the affirmative, as there was a tone of seriousness in her voice.

Five minutes later, an assembly of faces was projected on the view screens of the conference room.

Dr. O. called the meeting to order and set the stage.

"OK, here's the deal," she started. "We have to have an understanding of these energy pulses we are seeing and quickly. I need all available personnel, sensors, instruments and telescopes on this. I want the main frames dedicated to finding coherence or any signs of intelligence in these probes. Leave no stone unturned, answer every question, do not stop until the job is complete. I need an e-mail report every hour from your groups. The commander is very concerned about this and we need to give him an answer on one fundamental issue, is this energy hostile or not. Final report due in six hours. Now, lets get to it."

She was as serious as she was capable. All of the managers, scientists and engineers present respected her and knew her leadership would give them the best support they could get to find the answers to these questions. She was best described as the captain of the team, willing to work as hard if not harder than anyone else. Sleep was a secondary consideration. They broke off, mustered the technicians, mathematicians and support personnel to look at all aspects of the phenomenon.

What they found was as fascinating as it was disconcerting. There was a methodical effort to scan every emanation and absorptive quality of the great ship as it

37

approached the fifth planet in the star system. Although tenuous in many ways the energy probes delicately examined every aspect of the ship, from energy signal to construction materials.

"I think they are more curious than malicious," reported Dr. O. to the commander on the first of several telecons. "The beams explore us from the lowest of frequencies in the electromagnetic spectrum to the highest gamma ray levels we can detect. The probing is methodical and after several exploratory wide band sweeps, started paying particular attention to our computer clock frequencies and our communication frequencies."

The commander thought for a second, looked away from the teleconference camera, then looked back at Dr. O.

"We are still at a safe distance and can change course if needed, I am going to order preparations for that contingency but before we execute that maneuver, I want you to send a universal greeting on one of the frequencies these probes have shown interest in."

Dr. O. asked, "when would you like the message sent?"

"Immediately, the sooner the better," the commander said.

Dr. O. turned a bit from the camera, spoke at

38

another screen.

"Eric, send a universal greeting signal on the monitor channel and repeat it 60 seconds."

"You got it," a voice off camera said.

Within a few minutes the universal greeting signal was being broadcast, one that had several images imbedded in a digital code. The code also contained imbedded mathematical signatures to allow the interested to determine the level of sophistication in the creators of the message.

Forty seconds after the beginning of the broadcast, the probing signal from the fifth planet zeroed in on the antennas sending the signals and phased locked their emanations to the monitor frequency. After the message repeated itself 2.1 times the probe beams went silent. During the space between the next two broadcasts, the probe beams started to transmit another similar message, coded with a response to the universal greeting. It repeated itself in the silent spaces, waiting for either a change in the universal greeting or a response to their response.

"Ok, the message has been decoded and has very similar structure to our own message. They repeat certain components and add several of their own that we are now examining," Dr. O. reported.

"How soon will you have a more complete story," the commander asked, starting to relax a bit with the new found knowledge.

"We're on it full bore," said Dr. O. "the minute we get some answers I will contact you."

"Good."

Cathy got back to work with her team. Soon they discovered some more interesting facts about the probe beams. They emanated from several places on the surface, all had multi-spectral capabilities and at times they combined to add energy to their emanations. The energy signatures were never very high, enough to be able to receive and transmit, but not enough to do damage. They reminded some of the plasma tendrils in the neon globes from the late 20th century.

"Ok, what's the latest?" asked Cathy of her research staff, all on teleconference.

"They are sending us a bit of repeated greetings from us plus several images of their own, numerical messages based on their understanding of our alphabet, and some unknown symbols which we are guessing are a compressed series of words," reported Justin Walker, an able post doc in extra-solar civilizations. "We are working on the parts we do not fully understand right now on the

40

main computers."

"What can you tell us with confidence?" asked Cathy, a bit relaxed after an obvious major successful effort on her staff's part.

"Well, for starters they are fascinated with us and are asking about our culture, home planet, genders, food, entertainment, art and several other cultural attributes. They have also presented to us coordinates and images of a landing place. The images of themselves I can only describe as homogeneous, in other words they appear to have two genders like ourselves and offspring like our own, only they all dress very similarly and groom themselves in the same fashion," Justin said.

"How humanoid are they?" asked Cathy.

"Pretty much like ourselves, not reptilian like the last planet. As I said they are homogeneous, same shape, weight, bone structure, much less body hair, slightly larger eyes. They are in general shorter it seems with what appears to be larger cranial capacity. One interesting observation we had concerned a what looks like a piece of jewelery near their temples. This object is worn by all the people we think, certainly all of the ones in the images we have received. I assume its jewelery but I could be wrong, it

41

might be technology of some sort. The only reason I am thinking that is because if there is a change in the object of attention with one of them, they all seem to react or respond in unison. I'm just wondering if what appears to be jewelery does something more," Justin explained.

"Interesting, continue the analysis, send more details in the greeting, and open Data channel 0 for reception. Do not, and I repeat, do not, connect the Data Channel 0 receiver to the internal network. I will talk to the commander about restricted access to a small data set," Cathy O. said.

"Done."

Another researcher, Owen Smith, spoke up. "There is something else." he said. Owen was the radio astronomy team leader, able and intelligent, and certainly thorough.

"What did you find?" asked Cathy.

"We looked at the radio emissions from one Hertz to one Terahertz. Although the probe beam frequencies are generally distributed across the entire spectrum, we found an interesting stable pulsation at 3.1415926 seconds, pi of course. Their world is synchronized at this frequency, I think their communications and computational networks use this timing as an interrupt pulse to coordinate data transfer and power production, Owen said."

~The Voyages of Gaea~

Many years ago, Earth synchronized their computers and communications networks to such a degree that space probes looking back from millions of miles away could detect the one second pulsations of the power grids and communications networks as a result. Time had not been universal on Earth until the late 1800s, clocks were basically random. The need for sailors to know their longitude precisely and the need for the trains to keep from hitting each other required the creation of time zones, accurate clocks, synchronization and the Greenwich Meridian. Universal time or UTC was created as a result. As technology got more sophisticated and timing satellites, starting with GPS, were launched, the communications and data networks started to control themselves based on more and more accurately placed one second intervals. This evolved to the point of having these networks transfer energy from interrupts at a very exact time, thereby pulsing the energy grids at the same time. The result was that the Earth had a "heartbeat" that throbbed a significant amount of radio energy every second.

Owen continued, "The pulses from this planet are accurate from one to the next to within nanoseconds. We can infer from this that their level of technological growth has been very high, maybe more than our own."

43

"Thank you", said Cathy. "I will mention that in our next report to the commander. Lets open a channel and see what happens. And we should get together at the top of the hour."

The telecon was finished, the researchers went back to their instruments and Cathy sat down to consider the new information. Owen had brought up an interesting detail, intelligence included synchronization. There was information in the presence of data as well as the absence, if time is precisely known. Judging by the accuracy of their pulses, the energy distribution of their probes and their repeating of the universal greeting, Cathy wondered if this civilization was so advanced to be of a great concern. The only detail that slowed her from a dire conclusion was the sense that they appeared curious, maybe even desperately curious.

The commander elected to continue towards the new planet, elected also to open the Data Channel 0 to a limited data set containing many pictures, written works, star charts, and other scientific details. Within a few moments, the probe beams from L'quacious 5 found the available data and accessed it as quickly as electronically possible. They seemed voracious, as soon as all available data was transferred, a second transfer was attempted,

44

when the probes realized it was a repeat data set, there was a moment of silence, then a significant amount of return traffic was detected at a frequency exactly twice that of the Data Channel 0 frequency. The science crew and mainframe computers where overwhelmed for many hours trying to make sense of the new information.

Soon however the intent of the new planet's probings was determined to be non-hostile, in fact, it was determined to be incredibly desperate for more information. With the opening of the Data Channel 0, the inhabitants of L'quacious 5 learned the language enough to ask for more and more information on several particular subjects.

The commander selected which data were appropriate to send back to answer their inquiries. In all cases, the reply was a request for more.

Within several more weeks the Earth craft was within orbital range. By this time, "real time" communications were possible. The inhabitants visually appeared on many com channels, all asking (in a polite way) for more information about the travelers from afar. The commander gave what he deemed safe, never information about defensive systems, although they never asked for any.

During this time, it was determined that the pieces

of jewelry all of the inhabitants wore, were electronically connected to their version of the Internet, similar to the smart phones many of the away team members possessed. They had integrated their biological selves with their electronic creations at a very high level.

They were one with their technology.

The obvious benefit was instant access to information, they had implanted access points into their brains, allowing for a direct connection to their network of computers. They had understood and perfected the capabilities of their brains and as a result optimized their ability to gain knowledge.

This came at a price, however. They had stepped over a precipice with significant consequences, known as the law of unintended consequences.

The price was the loss of that non-specific component of being that concerns itself with art, music, love, smell, taste and wonderment of the existential. A heavy price by any measure.

The earth craft entered orbit, with full, comfortable communications with the civilization below. A landing place was determined and a landing team chosen. The carefully chosen team was made up of a significant amount of technologists, able to determine the level of sophistication in

46

this civilization. In addition, there was the resident philosopher, poet and sculptor. These people were sent to determine the level of cultural and intellectual achievement. Intellectual in the sense of literature, art and the understanding of the difference between existence and being.

They flew down in one of the shuttles, landed in a pristine and beautiful setting amongst the meadows and wetlands that had been allowed to flourish on their planet. It was obvious from distant observations that the world had been sculpted, engineered and its "nature" controlled. Significant amounts of energy was required to do this as they had discovered that the natural variations in meteorology was incompatible with their desire to optimize their environment. All flora and fauna were "managed." This was a "natural" outgrowth of their desire to dominate knowledge. The aggressive nature of their existence created a world of pure information and control.

Within seconds of their arrival, the landing party found themselves surrounded by a stunningly curious group of inhabitants. They closed in to within a few feet, examining the away team closely. A leader demanded, "tell us everything about your journey, everything."

Before the landing party leader could respond, the

47

same person continued, "tell us about all of you, every detail. Why are you so different? You come in many hues and shapes, you are many sizes, we have not experienced this."

The landing party leader interrupted, "We are..."

The reception committee stopped stone cold silent in anticipation of every word and stared, unblinking.

He continued, "we are pleased to be here, to meet you and we hope we have much in common. Now if you could show us to your governing council.....

"More, please...more," asked the landing party leader. They waited in breathless silence.

"Okay," continued the landing party leader, "we have landed here today to make first contact with you, we are from Earth, a planet many of your planet to sun distances away. We have observed your probe beams, anticipated your peaceful nature and look forward to a mutually beneficial interchange of information."

The reception committee leader and all of the colleagues present were waiting for more. They did not as it turns out receive any "information" and thus did not understand the landing party leader's response. They clarified the situation:

"How fast do you process data, how much data to

48

you posses?"

Sensing a discontinuity in intent, the landing party leader decided to take control of the situation.

"We can supply you with those answers, but we must talk with one of your leaders first."

"We are all leaders," was the reply. "We are all connected to the conduit and are all open to your inputs." The crowd looked intently at the visitors, did not blink or breath (it seemed). No one else spoke but their spokesperson, and drank in every nuance or inflection contained in the words of the landing party leader.

"Okay then," started the landing party leader. "Lets go somewhere and sit down to talk."

"Why?"

"We can give you more information if we are comfortable."

"We will make platforms for you, stand by.....the robots will be here in 3.2 bins."

The Terrans had learned on their way to the planet that its inhabitants based their lives on a binary system, cutting their orbit into factors of 2^n to define their time. A "bin" was $1/(2^{16})$ increments or about 2 minutes in Earth time.

Robots appeared in the appointed time period.

49

They quickly manufactured platforms with seat backs very near the landing shuttle. The inhabitants stayed in their positions, did not move and did not speak while the construction was in process. At the conclusion of the work, the robots left, the inhabitants moved to be equidistant from the Terrans, who, sensing the logic of the activities found their way to the seats.

"Thank you," the expedition party leader started. "We are from a planet much like your own, 12.8 light years away." He raised his arm to the sky and pointed in the approximate position of the Earth. "We have traveled here on a voyage of discovery over the last 21 of our years in search of other life in the universe. We detected your probing signals many months ago and as you know interacted with you and tried to answer your questions. It is our intent to find an efficient way to communicate with you for the benefit of both our civilizations. We notice that you have what we would call jewelery, all very similarly styled that all of you wear....."

"Those are our portals," said the closest L'Quation. Silence followed.

"And may I ask what their purpose is?"

"To be one with the central information. The entity that gives us information."

"Do all of your people wear such a device?"

"Yes. Do you have art, music and poetry?"

"Uh, yes we do," came the somewhat surprised reply from the away team leader.

"May we see your art, music and poetry?"

"Of course, do you not have these things yourselves?"

"They have no place in our information centric life, long ago our files were purged to allow more data. All we have is many references to these things, but no examples. We have found that our civilization was significantly different long ago, when they had these things. Since then, we have been the same."

More silence.

"Of course, we will share these things with you." the leader said.

"Can we have all of your art, music and poetry?"

"We will make arrangements to give you access to our files and if you would like, we can introduce you to some of our artists, musicians and poets."

"We will give you everything we have in return," said the L'quation.

"Oh, please, that won't be necessary. It would be our pleasure to share these things with you," the leader

51

replied.

Silence.

"Uh," the leader started, "I will begin making arrangements now."

"There is no balance," the L'quation began, "where there is give there is take, when there is up there is down, we give you platforms, you give us information. For such a thing as art, music and poetry we feel it is necessary to give you everything in return."

"I understand, we can talk about that later, first we would like some information; we would like to know about you, your history, your activities."

"Our history is simple, we were like you for many millions of orbits, we then evolved our technology to be equal to our personal capabilities and then more than us. A decision was made to accelerate our growth by integrating our technology into ourselves, to give us access to information at a much higher rate. 94% of our population is plugged into the information to such a degree that there is no need to do anything else, food and shelter is provided for us. Most of us stay at home, connected to the net. This small group you see here however, succumbed to a computer virus which changed our growth commands. The virus did not allow us to connect completely to the net. The result of which is that we were able to discover our past, our past as significantly different to who we are now. We thought for ourselves then, we had art, music and poetry. Now we do not need to think for ourselves, it is too archaic. For many many orbits, we have been unchanged and ungrowing. Once the control software was stable and considering how hard that was to accomplish, the version was frozen and the people here remained the same, not having a need to change. In the case of the small group before you however, we think for ourselves and talk amongst ourselves, which causes much confusion to our peoples and computers. Can you help us? We are alone here."

The landing party leader stood silent and a bit stunned.

"We can help you, we will first talk to our people in orbit, then make a decision."

The L'Quations stood silent, communicating between themselves and waiting for a decision from the visitors.

The leader decided to not make a hasty decision and evaluate what he had heard. It was getting near dusk now and the crew members could see the flickering lights of many visual displays in the L'Quations distant homes now that it was getting dark. The flickering was coincident, meaning that the inhabitants of this planet it seemed, watched the same channel. The same channel all of the time.

A researcher, Karen Kay, walked up to the leader, waited her turn to talk and said:

"Their starved."

"What do you mean?" asked the leader.

"Their starved for anything other than data, this civilization made the decision to integrate themselves into their highest form of technology, which was all computer based. That change modified their lives to such a degree that they cannot return to what we would call normalcy. The 'deviants' we see here are cognizant of a completely different civilization that proceeded them. If we give them what they want, they will be significantly influenced; our art, music and poetry represents the best and worst of our essence. The decision to give them these things cannot be made lightly. Our art for instance includes many works of beauty as well as works or the horror we perpetuated on ourselves during our most turbulent periods. Remember Guernica, which the L'Quations most certainly will discover, which shows the ghastly inhumanities we perpetuated during the Spanish War of Independence. Also, they might

54

not understand the impressionistic and expressive art forms. Would they mis-interpret these works? They, like our music and poetry resonate with us because we connect with where they are from. The subjects in most cases are contemporary to our history. We must be careful about the unintended consequences of our actions."

The expedition leader looked at Karen, thought for a while and replied:

"You're right, we must be careful. We most certainly would significantly change this world with our most personal expressions. I need to confer with the commander in orbit before proceeding."

The leader turned to the waiting L'quations and said:

"We need to confer with our superiors regarding your request. Your patience is greatly appreciated on this matter and we will return to tell you of our decision."

The L'quations stared unblinking at the leader and remained silent. One individual, after a long moment spoke:

"Please?"

The expedition group stood from their sitting platforms and moved towards the landing shuttle. As they cleared the area, the robots who originally made the structures returned and dismantled them, organizing the materials in neat piles for a return to their warehouses. The crew boarded the shuttle, went through a short pre-flight checklist and took off for the mother ship.

The trip took 45 minutes, during which time some crew members talked amongst themselves about their experiences on the surface. The majority of the crew including the leadership, remained for the most part silent. The trading of cultural gifts was common between different groups on earth. This would be different, whereby the gravity and import of a gift could have a significant impact on the recipients.

Once on board the mother ship, a conference was quickly convened to discuss the experiences of the initial expedition. "Recordings, notes and conversations were reviewed.

"What we have here is a careful decision that needs to made fairly quickly," said the commander. "What can we give these people to satisfy their curiosity and needs? On the one hand we are dealing with a special group of individuals that are anomalous to their society. Should we give tools (so to speak) to this group only?"

Silence met his words.

He continued, "Should we give them all a conduit of

information to all of our knowledge?" He paused again. "Well I need recommendations in four hours as to how to proceed. We will meet here again at six, top of the hour."

The commander turned back from looking at a clock on the wall as he said these last words. He had a look of seriousness that spoke volumes. No easy task, decide whether to help and possibly pollute or not help and confuse our new friends.

After six hours, the recommendations had been offered and considered. The commander went to his private office for a few minutes, after which he returned to the command center and summoned several individuals. After private and separate discussions, they all went to work behind closed doors.

The commander went to the comm station.

"Inform the L'Quations that we will be leaving their system soon. We have heard and will respond to their request in the next few days. The objects we will bring will take time to produce."

"Aye, aye, sir," replied the communications officer.

In the isolated areas where the select crew members worked, the pace was brisk, as they were under tight deadlines to complete their tasks in three days. 18 hour days where the norm and after the three day period alloted by the commander, their work was covered, boxed and sent to the shuttle bay for transport to the surface.

Soon the objects were secured in the largest shuttle, a select team of pilots was assigned and the flight plan written up.

On the forth day, the commander sent a message to the L'Quations again, telling them to return to the original landing spot. The shuttle had already flown to the landing zone, removed the gifts and prepared them for the inhabitants. After they were done, they flew back to the mother ship, informing the commander of the return flight.

The L'Quations returned in silent formation and found the following items:

A full size perfect replication of Michelangelo's Pieta.

The music of Vivaldi, Bach and Schumann in both written and recorded form.

The poetry of Gerrard Manley Hopkins, Frost and Aeschylus.

Replicated paintings from DaVinci, Picasso, Renoir, Monet, Kandinski and Pollock.

In addition there were several other interesting items:

Plato's Republic, The movie 'Casablanca' and the

recorded voices of the St. Petersburg Choir, Botticelli, Caruso and Pavarotti.

The final gift was a recorded message from the commander of *Gaea*.

"Greetings from the travelers of Earth. We leave these gifts in hopes of fostering a long and prosperous relationship. These gifts represent many historical perspectives in Earth's history. As that history is complex, we offer no explanation now for the interpretation of these objects. They are objects of creativity borne from the social environments of their respective eras. We leave them here for *your* interpretation, which is what we have decided as the most important aspect of our gifts. We shall return someday eager to hear of your impressions. In that respect, they will be more yours than ours. Beyond that point we will have a better understanding of how to pursue our burgeoning friendship. We must depart now to our next destination, but will keep our communications channels open."

The L'Quations stared in silence for hours at the gifts. They neither touched them or averted their eyes from the first object they individually found. Darkness fell, they all remained, initially bathed in the light of the same Milky Way that had looked upon the original sculptors, poets and writers. One of their two moons made its presence known and cast another light, another luster on the gifts left by the visitors. They continued to absorb the aura, not willing to leave the new surrounding, rife with new possibilities. Their souls remained agog for years.

Epilogue:

Contact remained with Gaea and the home planet Earth. Controlled by the masses of L'Quatious 5, the requests continually came in for more information Perturbations became evident however in the ensuing years, within the requests. A change in the tone of their words let the original Terranauts to the conclusion that their gifts had had an impact.

On the surface of the planet, the infected clan wrote, painted and morphed their surroundings to express themselves. The remaining inhabitants were unaware of the new order and eventually, faded into the past, much like old software.

THE OTHER END OF THE STORY

"Any sufficiently advanced technology is indistinguishable from magic"

-Arthur C. Clarke

~*The Voyages of Gaea*~

During the period of *Gaea's* voyage, large antennas on Earth, typically radio telescopes, where tasked with maintaining a link to the spacecraft. Most of the traffic was mundane, usually private family communications along with telemetry from the ship. There were requests for equipment and supplies that the telescope operators relayed to the *Gaea* command center. The amount of traffic was consistent and took up several hours a day to handle.

The telescopes were in use around the world to maintain a 24 hour coverage of the traffic, most of these were very large dish antennas and typically old. They were from installations and experiments created in the past and whose usefulness had waned. These radio telescope observatories where, after the end of their active periods, underfunded and manned mostly by volunteers. The labor costs were cheap, also, these volunteers had used parts and electronics of their own making or had "scrounged" from other pieces of equipment. As a result the reliability of these observatories was sometimes low. The worldwide interplanetary voyage project had provided some funds for upgrades and new equipment, but cost over runs and mismanagement caused much of these funds to disappear before finding their way to the working sites. The result of which was that the operators of these facilities were not

62

paid well, the equipment was basic at best and required constant attention and maintenance.

At the old amateur radio astronomy site in Colorado (the Deep Space Exploration Society), two 60 foot antennas were linked together and phase matched to create a single communications facility with the effective gain of a single 85 foot dish, just large enough to maintain good signal levels with *Gaea*.

A sole operator, Jason Codar, spent 12 hours at his station most every day, on a *sidereal* schedule, meaning that he went to work three minutes earlier every day. Over the course of a year, his schedule slipped a full 24 hours. Year after year he remained at his post, took a minimal amount of time off and relished the thought of being an important participant in the extra planetary mission.

On a typical schedule he would show up 30 minutes early to warm up and calibrate the equipment. The main components were a very accurate atomic clock, antenna control unit, receiver and transmitter. There were a few computers at hand to link to the internet and monitor the health of the system. For the most part it was a simple job; calibrate the system, move the large antennas to a particular point in the sky and start tracking. Some of the more sophisticated tasks necessary to track an interstellar object included compensating for the doppler shift as the ship accelerated and de-accelerated during its trip. These latter tasks were done by the computers, needing little intervention by the operator. Jason brought in books, got a degree on line and learned fly fishing over the years he operated the station. He was always present however for any problems and took ownership and responsibility for this important outpost of communications.

Years went by with little change in routine, the antennas creaked their way across the heavens, the data streams ran initially at many megabits per second, as the ship gained distance, the data rate had to slow down to compensate for the great losses of signal strength. All in all however the system worked fine, Jason did his job well and life went on.

One day however there was a change. Jason showed up for work at three a.m., opened the large metal door that led to the control room. He viewed the floor, thinking it needed to be cleaned and waxed again. Turning right, he passed the restroom hoping it had not frozen again in the brisk Colorado air, which at this time of the morning was near 20 degrees F. He shut the door, pulling it until it clicked. Several times over his tenure here, he had unwanted visitors, usually panicked raccoons or an occasional bird who would wander in to the building and be freaked out as Jason found a broom and guided them to the door. On rare occasions a human would appear, even though it meant they were trespassing. The visitors curiosity took over these people and they all asked a few questions and quickly left. Jason would be polite but clearly let them know he had very important work to do. He learned to lock the door behind him after too many interruptions. Jason moved from the parts room through the electronics lab to the operations control room. Looking right, he pushed the coffee maker 'on' button initiating the characteristic burbling sounds. Moving back to his left, he scanned the electronic instrumentation, quickly assessing if it was working in the same way as it had the day before. Satisfied, he placed his backpack near the chair and console he would occupy over the next many hours. Turning on the monitors, he waited for them to settle, casting an eye through the small window to the outside, he paused, somewhat dazed from his strange life cycle, and thought about the big ship out there, making discoveries on an almost daily basis. The people back home looked forward to the information coming back, especially about the new civilizations they had encountered and the detection of many more.

Jason turned back to the monitors. It was almost an hour before the communications channels could be opened, he decided to calibrate the system by looking at some pulsars in the general region of the spaceship. He called up a planetary program that showed the positions of (in this case) several pulsars in close proximity to each other. He placed the cursor over the first pulsar PS1919+21 and commanded the first 60 foot antenna to point in that direction. He thought for a second and decided to point the second 60 foot antenna in the direction of a second pulsar, within one degree of the first. The noises and creaks of both antennas interrupted the night.

It had been thought for many years that the variation in signals from pulsars, easily observable, where due to "interplanetary scintillation" or twinkling. Signals from the stars responsible for the pulsations varied quite a bit as observed from many, many observations over the years. It was assumed that the scintillation from the closely spaced stars would be much the same, insofar as the intervening space from the pulsars to the Earth was the same.

Jason had a unique opportunity to test that theory because he had two large antennas that could be pointed independently. He also had two receivers and two data

66

channels that could, in software be compared in real time. Over the last several months, Jason had prepared the software on his off time, just out of curiosity. He knew what the answer would be but wanted to verify it anyway.

The whirring came to a stop on one antenna, then the other, found its target. Fainter noises came out of the pedestals as the large antennas started to track their targets. Jason connected cables from each receiver to the backs of two data acquisition units. The receivers registered signal levels that were as expected, the variation in the signal level meters was evident in the bouncing of the needles. Interestingly, the bounces did not coincide. Jason thought about this anomaly for a second and decided that the electronics might respond at difference rates in each receiver, better let the more sophisticated computer programs make the more accurate measurements. He moved over to the control console and sat down.

For this measurement, he inverted one receiver output and added it to the non inverted second receiver output. In this way, if the signals were the same, the result would be zero or null. Within seconds of commanding the computer subroutines to perform this task, he viewed a graph on the monitor that caused him to stop breathing. The signals did not add up to zero, more remarkably, they added up to a syncopating, modulating pattern that was not even remotely expected.

Jason rose from the chair and started to pace, clockwise, around the floor of the control room.

"Ok, this is not good," he spoke out loud.

He looked back at the monitor and saw the repeating modulation pattern. He averted his eyes, thinking of the potential meaning of this discovery.

"Well, this is not a discovery yet, I have to verify that the equipment is working well and the computer software is making the right computations. First this..."

He went over to the receiver rack and reversed the cables between receiver A and receiver B. This would show if the data acquisition was faulty or even the software. Looking back to the monitor screen, he saw the same results.

"Rats."

Next he simply disconnected one receiver from the associated antenna and viewed the results, the screen showed the expected scintillation pattern. He did the same for the other receiver and got the same results.

"Rats."

By this time the spacecraft was in view and he needed to do his real work, connecting the stellar voyager

68

to the internet. The phone rang as he was putting the cables back in the original configuration.

"Hello?"

"Jason? Is there a problem? Your 16 minutes late to connect."

"No, no problem, just had a wind anomaly, we're connecting now."

"Ok, we have the signal up now, we might have lost a small portion of the first incoming message as it handed off from the East coast facility to you. Looks good, let us know if there are any other issues."

"Shall do, looks good on my end, talk to you later," Jason said, realizing that the operator on the other end would probably look at the wind reports from this site and find at best a two knot gust.

"Later," the voice said.

Jason, now a bit sweaty decided to cover his tracks by writing an e-mail to the operator on the other end to cover any dis-continuities. He would tell this person the truth, that he got caught up calibrating the system and missed his deadline.

"Now what," Jason muttered.

He sat down for a moment to monitor the displays and monitor screens, everything was working well. Leaning

69

forward he brought up the last recorded measurement from his two pulsar experiment. The pattern repeated, showing only minor differences from cycle to cycle. "Scary," he thought. "What on Earth is this?" The notion made him smile, this was not from Earth. This was interstellar. Rotating right, he opened a reference book which contained the distances from the Earth to many stars, galaxies, nova and pulsars. The two he had observed were near each other in space.

"Are they in some kind of resonance," he thought?

The data revealed there was synchrony and logic to the patterns.

"Something like.......like.......a radar. A Radar! What would two pulsars being doing, synchronized like a radar signature? The patterns, the patterns are like the radar signatures we used to probe the planets many years ago. A repeating pattern with minor changes, mathematical changes imbedded in the data streams. We used this to accurately judge the distance to the features on planets! Why? Why use pulsars? How do you control pulsars?"

Jason put the book down, got up for a walk and this time moved counter clockwise across the lab floor. After many minutes he came to a couple of conclusions: first he would have to get his findings verified, then he would need

70

to make more precise measurements on the signal he had discovered. He could not take any more readings until the next evening when *Gaea* was just below the horizon, 23 hours from now. That would be a long wait, but at least it would allow him to quiet down and carefully consider his options.

That day was a long one, the data transmissions went well, no loss of signals, the equipment stayed calibrated. He went home that evening, slept badly, woke up early and went back to the ground station. By this time the source had risen into the sky enough to be viewed with his antennas. Again, he viewed the same two pulsars with individual antennas, did the subtraction, saw the modulated patterns and again, got nervous.

He thought:

"This appears intelligent, designed, and purposeful. But why? Why put out a very strong signal that looks like a radar. There is no information imbedded into it other than a slowly repeating pattern, just like a planetary radar. It announces the presence of sentient beings, but to what purpose?"

He called his mentor, Jeff Keeler, for consultation. The cell phone rang a few times...

"Hello?"

71

"Jeff, this is Jason, out at the *Gaea* downlink station north of town, how are you doing?"

"Fine, Jason, good morning...my goodness, its early, anything wrong?"

"Well, Jeff, yes and no. The equipment is fine, downlinks are working well. Its just that during a calibration yesterday I discovered something interesting in the cosmos. Normally you would think that is should be very exciting, but this one give me pause."

"Sounds interesting. You sound nervous, shall I come over?"

"Actually, yeah, I would really appreciate it. Let me give you something to think about on your way over: The other evening, I placed each antenna on separate, closely spaced pulsars, initially for calibration purposes. I saw something odd in the data which upon examination indicates a coherence between the sources and a modulated signal when I differentiate between them."

"Scintillation?"

"No, I think I have ruled that out, there is a repeating pattern, like a long pseudorandom sequence the old Arecibo planetary radar system used to use. Very slow pulse repetition frequency as well, looks very similar."

"Wow, thats interesting. Have you ruled out

72

satellites?"

"The source tracks siderially, with the stars, its just weird that the two pulsars, which as I mentioned before, are close to each other in space, have signals that are so well modulated when viewed together. They each have different rotational periods that sets up a harmonic between them. But the added signal has a definite repeating pattern.

"Pseudorandom?"

"Yeah, repeating pseudorandom."

"I'll be right there. Sit on this until we can answer all of the questions that will get asked. Ok?"

"No problem, I'll sit on this."

"Ok, see you soon."

Jason, configured the antenna for the next telemetry run with *Gaea*, then waited for Jeff. It didn't take long as it was still very early in the morning and the roads were clear. The buzzer went off from the main gate within 25 minutes. Jason reached over and pushed the "Open gate" button. Another five minutes and Jeff was at the door of the lab.

"Well, lets see what you've got," said Jeff.

"Ok, here it is, individual signals from yesterday, signals from today, and their respective summations." answered Jason.

73

"Wow. This looks interesting. But first off lets eliminate some potential sources. Satellites?"

"No, checked the sidereal rate, available online resources, and NORAD"

"Local sources of interference?"

"Did an azimuth sweep of the area, even checked a few other co-located pulsars, nothing. The phenomena is connected to these two stars."

"So, that answers another question of mine. Ok, walk me through your data analysis." Jeff said, getting a more serious look in his face as the explanation was moving toward something that would get a lot of people excited.

They talked for several more hours, going over every detail several times. The conclusions were obvious, the analysis of the signal was legitimate. Now they needed an astronomer. The needed a very good astronomer, someone who knew the field of pulsar research with a good overview of high energy astrophysics. The first choice was Leslie Youngfield from Northeast Research Institute. She was a veteran of many observation runs, a good field astronomer and experienced in radio astronomical phenomena.

Now mid day, the telescopes were busy tracking

74

the spaceship and transferring data at a high rate. Jason and Jeff took notes, made careful measurements of the equipment's health and prepared to meet with Leslie. Luckily she was in town for a conference and had some time to meet. They decided on a time, rented her a car and went back to their chores.

After the spacecraft had moved below the horizon, the dishes were stowed in the vertical position, the electronics left on and the place cleaned up a bit. Jason and Jeff went outside, enjoying the sunshine and relaxing before the important visit. A long dust trail from the dirt road leading to the site announced the visit from the astronomer. A small SUV slowed to a stop, amidst a small swirl of dust, near the upper antenna. Leslie got out, grabbed a backpack and proceeded towards the awaiting engineers.

"Magnificent evening," she remarked.

"Beautiful, just beautiful," said Jeff, "thank you so much for taking time to talk to us. I know you are very busy but this signal has significant properties that you can help us understand. Jason has been very careful to calibrate the equipment and confirm the presence of this unusual signal. I tracks in a sidereal manner, has a repeating complex pattern and....

~The Voyages of Gaea~

"Walk with me," interrupted Leslie, as she put down her backpack, looked around for an isolated path across the mesa where the antennas were positioned. "This way."

Jason and Jeff looked at each other, then back to Leslie, who had a very serious, if not stern look on her face.

"Sure," was their reply.

Leslie started walking in a direction that moved them away from the mesa's edge, toward the center of the plateau and said nothing for 15 minutes. Jason and Jeff followed, glancing at each other periodically in their concern about what she was about to tell them. They reached an open spot, probably from a dried up pond, Leslie looked at the ground with some interest, then carefully viewed the horizon in a methodical circular movement. Finally, she addressed her companions.

"There are a few things I can tell you and many things I cannot. The Defense Department if fully aware of these signals, which we found a while back and two others we surreptitiously found a few weeks ago. There is significant concern about these signals as one, directed toward another planetary system, increased in power to such a degree, that the inhabitants, if any, would have been severely effected. The signals, we think, are from the pulsars, like the ones you found, and are modulated much

76

like a transistor or vacuum tube from some unknown source 90 degrees from the source of the electromagnetic energy. Theoretically, according to the Department of Energy's supercomputers, a much smaller amount of directed energy at a point orthogonal to the output stream, towards the pulsar, can modulate this stream in such a way as to use it as a radar beacon, or in the case of the planet I mentioned, as a very high intensity destructive beam.   The level of radiation on that planet was intense and directed carefully. We do not know what the purpose of the directed beam is but considering if that beam had been pointed at us, it would have boiled the oceans and caused an instant fire storm on the continents.   The government of the few nations who know about this are very concerned."

As she took a breath, Jason asked, "there are more pairs? How did they find them?

"I can't go into great detail now, suffice it to say that there are several more pairs, mostly in the same area of the sky. How they were found is classified, there are facilities like your own here (she motioned to the stowed upper dish) that you are familiar with and a few that you are not. Both of you now have to be cleared by the National Security Agency and FBI before we can continue. Lets go back to your facility.   Not a word of this conversation shall take place in there, at your homes, or anywhere else, is that clear?"

Jason and Jeff nodded, they all started back to the control room, quietly.

When they arrived, Leslie looked around the room, spotted the control computers and, looking at Jason, said:

"Take this thumb drive, load all of your data on it, run the program on the drive called "purge" after the data transfer, do not record any more signals and I will call you in two days."

"Of course," Jason said. He took the memory stick and did as he was told. Jeff meanwhile was just listening, smart enough to know that questions were not a good thing to ask right now.

"This is very commendable work you guys have done here, thorough and precise. Well done, I wish we could just get some champagne and celebrate, but we have a big problem to resolve before that."

Leslie took the thumb drive from Jason, walked towards the door, looked back with the same serious look as before.

"Not a word!"

She was out the door before either Jason or Jeff could respond. Silence followed for a minute, then Jason simply said:

"Wow."

"Wow is right."

"Nothing to do but continue the routine."

"Yep, lets wait for her call, I need to get back to work."

"Thanks for your help, Jeff, I think."

"My pleasure, don't worry about this until we know more."

"Got it."

Jeff left Jason, silent and looking at his equipment.

After about 30 minutes, Jason came out of his thoughts, turned off the non-essential pieces of electronics, walked out of the control room and locked the main door behind him. He got in his car, looked around for spies and started the engine. He felt he needed to get out of the area quickly, the antennas would guard their secrets well, until they were allowed to listen again.

On his way home, his mind raced with the developments of the day. His driving was imperfect, his concentration erratic. The drive was about 30 minutes through mainly rural areas, some dirt roads and generally low traffic, which was good, especially today. He took a right turn onto a paved road about half way home. His cell phone rang, he looked at the display.

"Its Leslie," he said to no one as the car drifted off of the road and the right wheels sank into the soft shoulder. He corrected the drift, slowed to a stop and answered the phone.

"Hi, Leslie."

"Jason, we are sending two technicians out to your site, they will be there within four hours. Please meet them at the main gate, I took a GPS reading of the position for them to use. They have your cell number and will call you when they arrive. Train them on the *minimal* operational requirements of your equipment. When you are satisfied they can handle the tasks, go to Buckley Air Force Base, where a government jet will be waiting for you. When you get to the guard shack, call me at this number and I will coordinate the rest of your visit here."

"Here?"

"You'll see. Now these technicians are very bright, tell them only what they need to understand how to continue the communications with *Gaea*. They know nothing else of what's going on, tell them you have a family emergency, tell them nothing more. Ok?"

"Ok."

"See you tonight, all of your arrangements will be

80

taken care of," she hung up.

Jason sat in the idling car for a while, decided to go home for a bit, gather a few things in his backpack and return to the antenna facility. In a way, he did not want to go back, for this facility now was part of some horrendous story. It held secrets known by the few, that could effect the many.

"Too much power," he thought.

Back in his apartment, he gathered some essentials for travel, a few books for reading and wondered, as he stood in the kitchen, if he was going to be back here anytime soon. Presently, he took his backpack, slung it over his shoulder and went out the front door. He turned to lock it, did so, then back to walk towards his car. A new car, with two people in it was parked a hundred feet or so from his own. This was out of place.

"I'm just paranoid," he thought.

He walked down the stairs, across the lawn of the apartment complex, towards his car. As he got close and reached for the door handle, the new car opened up its two doors. Two people, a man and a women, got out. They were dressed professionally, had the proverbial sunglasses on and looked initially at Jason. The women walked towards the apartment building's office, the man towards

81

Jason.

Jason froze, this was surreal. Was he in danger? He stood there helplessly as the man approached.

"On your way back?" the man asked.

Not knowing how to respond, Jason simply said, "Yes."

The man opened his jacket slightly to reveal a golden badge of some sort.

"Good, we will take care of everything here, Jason, have a good trip."

The man retracted into the black car, Jason got into his, now very nervous and drove back to the antenna facility. On his way, Jason's heart pounded, not knowing what was going on, only that serious people knew about his every move. The road back was again difficult to navigate, Jason periodically looked out the window for helicopters or the glint of binoculars. He saw nothing but knew they were there, probably following him with satellites.

He made it back to the antenna facility in due time, thankful to hear the main gate close behind him, although he knew it probably would not keep certain people out. He drove up the hill to the top of the mesa, turned left onto a dirt road and made the dust fly on the way to the control room as he had done so many times before. At the facility, he got out of the car, opened the building and waited for his replacements.

Within three hours, there were two people at the gate, he let them in and led them to the facility.

"Mums the word," he thought.

The two people who showed up were serious and insisted on getting the job done in an efficient manner. Very few pleasantries were exchanged as they has been taught that this was a serious mission and Jason was a very important person, one who they needed to relieve for a very special reason. They took notes, asked the right questions and gave Jason the distinct impression that they could do the task.

Jason left two hours after their arrival, confident that the data link to *Gaea* would not be interrupted. Confident yet he had that qweezy feeling about heading to the Air Force Base wondering what was in store for him.

The ride took a little over an hour, he relaxed a bit, listening to the radio and looking at the scenery like a new soldier getting ready to ship out from his home city.

"Wonder how long it will be before I return?"

F-16 fighters doing pattern work announced the fact that he was close to the base. Although this base was at the edge of a large city, the view beyond the barbed wire fence was like a different world. Large domes housing large antennas were set in a line, each surrounded by a fence and each guarded by German Sheppards and machine guns. There were quite a few buildings without windows which were also heavily guarded.

He drove down the western side of the complex, turned a corner to the north, followed the fence line until he saw the main entrance. There were barriers starting 50 yards away from the guard shack. He slowed the car down to negotiate the turns required to get to the checkpoint position. Heavily armed guards were sprinkled everywhere. The first few noticed that his car did not have the appropriate tags and stickers for a military person; they paid attention and followed the car with their eyes. It was obvious they were ready for anything. As he got closer to the check point, he passed a couple of bullet proof glass slabs that had been placed close to the area where the military guard was waiting.

Jason pulled up to the designated area, painted with a white stripe and just before the crossing gate which was in the down position. He stopped the car, put it into park and looking to his left saw three guards in uniform, armed, looking at him through a bullet proof window. One came out, approached the car and addressed Jason.

84

"ID please."

"Sure, here you go."

The other two guards slipped out of the guard shack, moved around the back of the car, one came over to the passenger side.

"Sir, could you open the trunk."

The guard quickly disappeared and moved to the back of the car, the other guard had been inspecting the underside of Jason's car during this time. Jason reached over and pulled the trunk latch to open the lid. As he moved the first guard followed his every movement. Someone else was inside the shack, checking the driver's license. After a moment, something was said to the first guard, he turned back to Jason.

"Sir, park the car over there, someone will be there to meet you." The guard pointed to an open place on their parking lot, just beyond the gate.

Jason, looking at the sidearms and automatic weapons the guards had, observing their very serious demeanor, thought for a second and said:

"I'll bet you throw like a girl."

The guard, un-amused, didn't flinch or miss a beat.

"Right over there sir."

Jason drove his car to the appointed place, shut

down the engine, got out to retrieve his things and raising his head, found he was looking at an officer, who said:

"We'll take care of these things, just come with me please."

Jason got into a nondescript Ford of some sort, in the back in fact, and while the door was shut for him, looked back at his car, which by now had military people going through it and wondered again what was in store for him. He wondered also about meeting that guard again.

The car took off toward the center of the base, took a few turns, came into another parking lot near the control tower at the center of the airfield and stopped. The officer got out, Jason waited until he was let out. Looking at the officer, he asked:

"Do you know what....."

"In due time sir, please follow me."

He was led through the terminal building, with many military personnel present. Several of them looked up and followed Jason's movements through the hallways to an open area, where there were several metal detectors and x-ray machines.

"Take off any metal objects, place them in this bin. Shoes and coat as well."

It wasn't like a commercial airport, much less

politeness here.

Jason went through the various machines, was led to a special room and was further probed with a wand and patted down. His coat and other belongings came in several minutes later.

"We have taken your cell phone and laptop, you will get them when you are done. Your apartment has been packed up and your belongings will be sent to a new place, not sure where yet. Follow me, sir."

"Ok...."

Jason emerged from the pat down room, looked around and followed the officer out to the tarmac, up to a slick looking private jet, door open. He climbed the stairs, looked to his left to find a flight crew going through a pre-flight check list. He looked right to find another officer in the aircraft, with more accoutrements on his uniform. He moved to sit opposite of the officer, in a comfortable looking first class seat.

"Hello," Jason started.

"Jason, have a seat, we will be leaving in a few minutes," the officer paused as the first jet engine started spooling up.

Another person, military but not an officer, appeared, pulled the door shut and secured it, he turned to the flight crew, said something to them and found an empty seat in the front of the aircraft. With one engine stabilized, the jet started to move, the other engine was started as this happened. Within what seemed to be just one minute they had taxied out to the active runway. Jason saw the captain push the throttle up towards the instrument panel and with seconds felt the g forces mount as they very quickly gained speed. Jason squeezed the arm rests, the captain pulled back the control column about three inches and the jet seemed to blow off the runway. This was followed very quickly by a steep left hand turn, then wings level, nose very high and airspeed increasing quickly. Jason heard the aircraft radio:

"Juliet Papa three, no speed restrictions during climb out."

"Roger, no speed restrictions."

"Juliet Papa three, turn right to one one zero, cleared direct Houston."

"Right to one one zero, cleared direct to Houston, Juliet Papa three."

The jet banked slightly right, still full throttle and climbing like a Banshee. Jason looked out the window and saw that the angle of the wing relative to the horizon was at least 30 degree, probably more. He looked over towards the officer across the isle.

The officer said, "We are going to get you there quick, no restrictions and the traffic has been cleared. Nothing like the royal treatment, eh?"

"Man, this jet is moving like nothing I have ever experienced before, how fast are we going?"

"Point nine seven when we level off, we should be there in a little over an hour. Want anything to drink or eat?" The officer unbuckled, even as the jet was screaming through the sky, got up and went forward to the galley. On his way there, Jason replied:

"Diet coke please, what kind of food do they have on board?"

"Diet coke it is," he looked toward the other person on board, "Steward, give the man a menu."

The steward came back with a menu, handed Jason a drink and waited. The jet was still at a high angle of attack, screaming through the sky. Jason looked over the menu, the jet's nose started to lower to a more level pitch, the speed started to increase as was evident by the increasing air noise across the fuselage.

"Filet Mignon, please."

"Right away, sir." The steward moved back forward, passing the officer on his way back to the seat. There were a few bumps, enough to light up a commercial jet's seatbelt sign. This jet had those signs, but they never were illuminated. The jet increased speed some more, then Jason observed the Captain pulling back the throttles just a little bit. A few switches were thrown on the instrument panel and the autopilot took over the flying duties.

Jason looked over to the officer.

"Good pilot, huh?"

"Ex Air Force One, she's got skills. Four combat tours, pilot instructor for Top Gun, astronaut wings, PhD in aerodynamics."

Jason raised an eyebrow, "any Cessna time?" He smiled.

The officer, detecting the bad joke, looked at Jason with steady eyes.

"This aircraft we're on *is* a Cessna, a Citation 12, capable of Mach flight, fully aerobatic with a few offensive and defensive toys we are not going to talk about. You see that seat belt light illuminate, buckle up quick, because we soon will be taking enough g forces that your eyeballs will be stuck to the ceiling."

"Got it," Jason said sheepishly.

"And don't piss off the military police again, they're here to take care of you."

"Ok, sorry about that," Jason said, wondering how that little tidbit of information had made it to the gentleman next to him.

"Alright, now that we got that straight, lets get down to business. Your here because you found something, something important. We have talked to your friend Jeff and assured him everything is in order. You on the other hand will get different treatment as your recordings Leslie took the other day held some more surprises."

"Ok." Jason said, keeping it short out of respect.

They spoke for a another 30 minutes as the jet screamed through the air in a direct path to Houston. The darkness of the sky indicated that they were at a high altitude, maybe 50,000 feet or so.

"So we will land very soon and transfer to a waiting V-22 Osprey."

"The tilt rotor used by the Marines?"

"That's the one," the officer said, looking out the window as the jet pitched over, the engines coming back to zero thrust.

Jason finished his meal, cinched up his seatbelt and looked out the window as well, not very comfortable with the significant nose down pitch. It had been a straight line from just about the beginning to end of flight, with a rushed meal

91

in between. He felt light in the seat as the jet was falling out of the sky at a rapid rate. Soon, they banked smartly left, the nose came up, landing gear extended and they quickly touched down. Rolling to a stop, the jet exited the runway about mid field. The aircraft taxied quickly on the tarmac, it seemed that the area had been cleared of personnel and equipment. Jason looked forward to see the captain's deft manipulation of the throttles. Within what seemed like 30 seconds, the jet taxied up to and beside a V-22 Osprey, sitting by itself on an open expanse of tarmac. The pilots and crew chief were waiting by the aircraft and started moving towards their places when the Cessna pulled up. The door opened, the steward got out and stood by the side of the door awaiting the emergence of the special passenger. The officer got up and followed Jason to the door. Jason looked back for a moment, about to say something but the officer quickly said:

"We need to move quickly, sir."

The officer pointed to the open door as Jason turned back forward and moved to the opening. He exited, smelled the fresh Houston air and without prompting, started to walk toward the V-22.

This machine was still ahead of its time, even after 30 years of service. Two very large propellers hung on nacelles at the end of each wingtip. Now tilted skyward, they would rotate in flight towards the front to provide 2,000 shaft horsepower each of thrust, enough to propel the craft to 360 miles per hour. The tail of the aircraft had a ramp for an entrance. Jason walked in the direction of the opening, accompanied by the officer. They walked in silence. As they approached the ramp, the crew chief appeared and started to walk toward them. The pilots had already entered the Osprey and started the pre-start checklist. The auxiliary power unit started up and the beacon started to flash as Jason and the officer entered the craft. The crew chief addressed them:

"Lets get inside, while you are getting buckled in I'll give you a flight briefing."

Jason and the officer moved amidships and sat down in two facing seats. They found not only lap belts but shoulder harnesses as well, indications of a more interesting ride ahead. The crew chief addressed them again:

"The most remarkable part of this flight will be the acceleration and the de-acceleration. Be prepared for it, tie down all gear well and brace yourselves. We will start out in a hover, then transition to forward flight, at about 200 feet above the ground, the nacelles will transition to their most forward position, where you will experience several g's for a moment. We will go from 20 miles per hour to over 300 in a matter of seconds."

The crew chief walked toward the rear of the craft, pushed some buttons to close the rear ramp, plugged in his headset and sat down in a special high g crew seat. He buckled up and cinched his belts tightly, a clue for Jason and the officer.

Jason quickly buckled in, pulled the straps tight as the engines were started in sequence. The large rotors came to life and started spinning quickly. Looking right, Jason watched the cockpit crew ready the aircraft for flight. The internal noise grew as the large props started taking a bite out of the air. The aircraft grew light and in a moment was hovering about three feet off of the ground. The Osprey turned about 90 degrees, started to air taxi, then continued to rise away from the ground. Jason could feel himself get heavier as the craft increased its altitude, then suddenly it seemed, the rotors started to rotate forward and the aircraft gained speed very quickly. Jason and the officer felt g forces sideways to their bodies for about 10 seconds then, looking out of a window, it was obvious that they were now moving at a significant speed. Still about 1000 feet off of the ground, the Osprey shot towards its destination.

In about 15 minutes, the sound level started to wane, followed by a perceptible de-acceleration as the rotors moved aft. The aircraft took a right turn, gear came out and they found themselves a mere 20 feet off of the ground at another aerodrome facility. Slowed to maybe ten miles per hour, the craft lined up on markings painted on the tarmac and rotating slightly lighted upon the ground like an eagle coming to its nest.

"That was amazing," Jason exclaimed.

"Fun ride, huh kid." the crew chief said passing by to talk to the cockpit crew.

The rear ramp was coming down as the engines spooled down. Switches were thrown, lists checked and within two minutes the Osprey was quiet. Jason and his companion got up and moved toward the ramp. Walking out and away from the V-22, the officer spoke:

"Ok, here's the drill, Leslie and several other people are waiting for you in a conference room, 3rd floor, main hallway, room 301. The guards have cleared you already and have a badge for you. Wear the badge at all times while at this facility, someone will stop you if you don't. I will take care of you when you are finished today."

"Thanks," was the reply.

"No problem, see you later."

The officer took a left turn as Jason went straight toward the main entrance of a five story brick and glass building. Going through the main door, he found his way to the guard desk, where several uniformed guards with guns were sitting and looking at him. One immediately went to a computer terminal while the second asked Jason for ID. Papers were produced requiring several signatures, mostly about understand the responsibilities for obtaining secret information. A picture was taken, as well as fingerprints and a retinal scan. The process took at least 20 minutes, after which a new plastic badge with and RF tag imbedded in it was produced. Jason clipped it on his shirt.

"You need to wave it in front of the designated boxes near the entrance doors. You are restricted from going into areas other than the ones we have discussed. Any problems call the guards at 511. Also, in several of the meeting areas you will be in, you will need to leave your cell phone, if you have one, at the door, there are shelves near the doors for this purpose. Have a good day."

Jason went through the lobby doors, which required the badge, then to the elevator, which required the badge, then to the hallway access door, which required the badge, then to the conference room, which required the badge. He had already had his cell phone confiscated.

Back at the entrance to the building, a computer took note of Jason's movements and final destination. The increase in Jason's security cost him his privacy.

Through the conference room door Jason went, he looked around and viewed a large long table, projector and screen at one end, conference phone in the middle and white boards on all walls. There were 12 people present and waiting for him. One open chair, he took it and sat down. Leslie was near the projector and spoke first.

"Thank you for coming Jason, I'm sorry but we needed you quickly. Also, I was a bit stern with you the other day, its based on the urgency of our 'problem' not a reflection on you."

"Its ok, I understand," said Jason, "It was quite a ride here, I feel like I left 20 minutes ago."

"Just a consequence of the speed and urgency," said Leslie, "lets get down to business. First off, nice job finding the radio source, good diligence along the way. Getting Jeff involved was a good move as well, he as you know works with me on various projects. I can say in this case that you went the more intelligent route as apposed to letting this thing go public. The President wants us to get all of the facts straight before he makes a speech on it."

"The President?"

97

"Yes, as it turns out you found a source of radio energy that we have known about for some time. It is of great concern to us because your measurements revealed something our facilities had not picked up. Using two antennas at the same time was the key and the interplay of the signals you found gives us more information about the source."

Leslie, after a short pause, continued, "Last year when we first discovered these signals, we alerted the engineers on *Gaea* about the details and asked them to use their Shoemarkian array to get more details."

Jason interrupted, "Shoemarkian array?"

Leslie continued, "Yes, this is an array of RF sensors which receive signals from any angle simultaneously, it was designed by a rogue antenna designer many years ago; basically it revolutionized antenna array design from RF through gamma ray frequencies by allowing no position in the sky to go unobserved. The data throughput of this device is immense as you can imagine and the dedicated computers on board the spacecraft are sometimes taxed when there is a fully bandwidth run. So, as it turns out that unbeknownst to you, your facility sent the signals, encrypted of course, to the ship about a year ago, considering the distance the ship is

98

now, we should be hearing their response any day now. Your discovery was propitious insofar as it gave us more information to add to that coming from *Gaea*."

"Glad to be of help, but what does it mean?" asked Jason.

Leslie responded, "We have theories and theories only. I mentioned to you when I visited your facility that we had observed a very large increase in energy from one of these beams, directed at a particular planet. I should also say that if we can observe these particular pulsars then they can direct such a beam towards us. Why they do this is not understood, that they have the capability to blow off a planet's atmosphere is. Needless to say, we are in range if they so choose to fire this thing. The powers that be have chosen to observe these beams on a 24 hour basis, looking for anything that might help us understand the origins and intelligence behind it. They have also chosen to craft a signal back towards these pulsars in an attempt to let them know there is life here. There are those who are concerned that when we make this transmission, it might not be interpreted as a friendly gesture but only as a new target designation. As you can imagine, we have had some very heated debates, including some serious discussions about making several *Gaea* like ships and moving people out of harm's way."

The other people in the conference room looked grim and remained silent. Some looked worn out from the intense debate that had taken place here and elsewhere over the last many months. It was obvious that a death ray could be headed towards us already. The main issue was to understand why a civilization would blow away atmospheres of worlds. It would have been helpful to understand what was going on with these other planets before the "cleansing."

Jason asked, "Do we have any archival information on the planets these death rays have hit?"

"We have some," a member of the conference room spoke up, "we have some spectroscopic information about one of the worlds, Hubble had viewed it many years ago but at that time the object of that Hubble search was not this particular phenomenon and therefore the data was just archived. The data provides more questions that answers as the atmosphere of this particular planet had significant amounts of heavy metals and most likely radioactive components in it. We can only guess as to why these elements were present, but the abundance was high and if any life was present on this world, it would have been significantly effected by this."

"Interesting, well as you all probably know, the Bikini Atoll, even after several nuclear blasts, still came back to life, except some Nurse sharks were genetically altered permanently."

"True, but we are jumping to conclusions here, we have no information about the history of these worlds, whether they are inhabited or not," another member of the room said.

Jason continued, "Was there a Shoemarkian array on earth that might have some archival information?"

"Don't know, we will look into it however." the same member said, while another member started typing on a laptop, presumably to initiate the search.

"And, I'm sorry, when do you expect to hear from *Gaea?"* Jason asked.

"Any time now," Leslie said, "for now we are scouring the old data for clues and are hoping that we aren't in the cross hairs."

Leslie sat back in her chair, looking at Jason, maybe for answers.

She then said, "for now we all need to stay close to this building, Jason, arrangements are being made for you. Any conversations outside of this room require Q level clearance, that of course, Jason, means that we do not talk

101

to anyone about this unless we are with cleared personnel inside a cleared facility, like this room."

"I understand."

"Ok then, we will keep everyone posted, Jason, someone will take care of you and is waiting in the main lobby."

"Got it."

The meeting broke up and people started to scatter. Leslie gathered her things and walked over to Jason, who, not having brought much in, had stood and was about to go out of the door. Leslie stopped him.

"Jason, a moment please."

"Of course."

They moved to the side to let everyone else out. Window shades were opened revealing a sunny day outside, with a few scattered clouds.

Leslie spoke.

"There are some very bright people here working with us in this room. They are exhausted from working this problem. We have looked at everything and considered every angle, but with no real conclusions. The information you received, in the way that you received it however, might be the key in understanding this beam."

She sat on the edge of the conference table,

relaxed a bit and waited for the last of the people to leave the conference room.

"The President is losing patience with us, we've known about this for some time now, the new information will help the situation, but not for long. If we don't hear from the spaceship soon, a decision of some sort will be made and that could go in one of many directions. Its imperative that you go over our data as well as review your own to find anything we might have missed. So for now you will live at this base and will have access to our equipment and computers. I suggest you don't stray very far, the guards will come and get you if you do. Oh and by the way, they don't throw like girls, even though many are women, they are highly trained and believe me, can take care of any situation that arises."

"How did you find out about that?" asked Jason incredulously.

"Jason, this is a hot topic, all eyes and ears are on this, show some respect and get to work."

"Got it. But you gotta understand, two days ago I'm concerned about interesting signals, now my apartment is empty, no one knows where I am, I just had rides on state of the art aircraft, so please excuse me for being moody."

"I hear you, we all have stories like that, its the price

of being popular."

Leslie looked at Jason, neither spoke for a bit, then she said:

"Someone is waiting downstairs for you, they will get you fed and set up at the dorm."

"Thanks."

She stood, looked for a moment out of the window. Jason thought for a moment.

"She looks like she misses the outside."

At that moment a person came into the conference room, with several papers in his hand, he went directly to Leslie.

"We have a response from *Gaea.*"

"Excellent, gather the troops," she said.

The aid left immediately, Leslie read the report the aid had given her before he left. She read silently, sometimes moving her lips. She then looked at Jason.

"The Shoemarkian array has acquired the signal very strongly, they are closer to the pulsars than we are and don't have to contend with the perturbations of a solar wind. I'll go over this in detail once everyone returns, but I can tell you this, they just got started."

Leslie and Jason found their seats again as the original members of the conference started to re-appear.

Aware of something important, they came in one by one, looked at Leslie, looked at the new papers in front of her and wondered what was next. Within ten minutes, everyone was back, Leslie rose to address the group and it became quiet.

"Thanks for coming back on such short notice. We have received the first response from *Gaea*. They have the signal and are now examining it in detail. Here is the transcript of the message we received an hour ago:"

-With regards to signal acquisition, pulsars, we have good signal to noise ratio and concur with you regarding the modulation. The Shoemarkian array is on it full time with a dedicated main frame computer. No conclusions yet except that they are using ranging tones and have now received reflected signals from *Gaea*. Will report every 24 hours until matter resolved. Matt Hyatt, Senior Scientist.

Leslie put the paper down on the table, looked up and said,

"More tomorrow, lets reconvene here at the same time. For now lets keep working and try to find an answer to this problem."

Leslie left before the others, probably to another meeting.

"She's a great manager," one of the team members

105

said to Jason.

"Yeah, I can tell, you people are lucky. She seems have a complete command of what going on. Its beyond competence, its about inhaling the situation and exhaling the truth."

Jason got up. "Well, see you tomorrow, I am off to the lobby to find out about my immediate future."

"Have a good evening," was the reply.

Jason went downstairs, back to the lobby, again through the electronically keyed doors. He noticed that if he approached slowly the computers had time to look up his access rights and open the door. Once in the lobby, he found a person waiting, who stood up in greeting.

"Jason?"

"Yes, thats me."

"I'm Susan Daley, I work for Leslie, we have a car outside for you and have brought your things into an apartment on base."

"Fabulous."

Susan gave him a quirky look then led him outside. They walked to the car in silence. She opened the passenger door for him and walked around to the drivers door. Once inside, she addressed him.

"Jason, I know that this has been hard for you and

106

we appreciate your patience on this matter, as you know we need your help. Your information was crucial and we would like you in the decision process during this period."

"I was uprooted. How long am I going to be here?"

"We know we moved quickly but it was imperative. As far at the length of your stay, as soon as the problem is resolved, you'll be free to go, but with some restrictions."

"What restrictions?"

"Much of what you will experience here is classified. You signed papers this morning that allowed us to do a full background check and give you a clearance. You must abide by the rules of that privilege under penalty of law.

"Sheesh," Jason responded, "the last few days have been a whirlwind. Two days ago I was examining an interesting phenomenon, thinking about its origin and makeup, now I am on a military base with a clearance and part of a confidential process, its a little unnerving. My life has been permanently changed. And now you tell me I must abide by the rules of a privilege afforded to me a few hours ago. What kind of rules?"

"The rules are simple," Susan began, "you may not discuss anything we do here with anyone unless they have established the 'need to know.' What this means is that you may not talk to anyone unless Leslie authorizes it. For the

107

most part who these people are will be obvious, but in the outside world, that means no one. This also means that all secure conversations will take place only in secure venues, like the conference room you were in a few minutes ago. No conversations in the hallway, outside or at home."

"Ok, that makes sense, at this point I have no information I want to share anyway."

"One final thing, if you get the feeling that someone is asking you questions you should not answer, you need to call this number (she handed him a business card), someone will show up who will be in plain clothes and act like your friend, you will introduce him to the person asking questions and we will take it from there."

At this point, Susan started the car and began the drive to the apartment Jason would stay in for the near future. The drive took about 10 minutes through the tree lined base, taking a few turns to a multi-story building somewhat nondescript, which was an apartment complex for visitors. She turned into the parking lot, wheeled the car into a space, placed it in park and shut off the engine. Jason looked at the entrance, saw a few people going in and out and noticed the distinct lack of communications between the inhabitants. They got out of the car, Susan led Jason into the lobby area where she made the

108

arrangements for his stay, obtained a key, turned to look at him and said:

"Have a good evening, your things are in your room, including a new cell phone, use that one only. Unless we call you tonight, please meet us at the same room tomorrow at 0900. There is a shuttle available, coordinate with the person at the front desk."

"Ok, thanks."

Susan turned and left. Jason looked at his key, noted the room number and walked to the stairs. After several flights, Jason emerged from the stair well onto a hallway, much like a hotel, medium lights to save energy, quiet demeanor, floral pattern on the rug. Down he walked about 50 feet until he found his room, opened with his key, walked in and shut the door. The room smelled a bit musty or maybe it was mildew, and it was a too warm. He found the temperature control, turned it to 72 and engaged the air conditioner. It had a television, small kitchen, queen size bed, desk and small balcony. The size was something like one and a half hotel rooms, an apartment barely.

After a quick look around, it was time for a walk to consider his situation, and to find some food. Jason changed his shoes in to something more comfortable and left the room, making sure the door was locked and walked down the hallway towards the stair well. Descending then emerging into the lobby, he went over to the desk clerk and asked about places to eat. "One mile to the East" was the response. Out the main door and looking at the sun (not totally believing the hand motions of the clerk) found his way East, down a nice road. The temperature in Alabama (he had just realized his final destination was Huntsville) was warm and the humidity high. The walk started by crossing the road and getting on a sidewalk, which had cracks and evidence that it had been there a long time. Looking to his left he found several small but nice houses, old it seemed, maybe even 1940's. Considering where he was, he imagined Operation Paperclip, where German rocket scientists were brought first to Ft. Bliss in Texas then eventually to this place, destined to design rockets and capsules that took people to space, the moon, and beyond; the seminal group of engineers and scientists, whose accomplishments were admired for decades.

"How could they do so much without cost and schedule overruns?"

Thinking about it further and looking at their closely spaced houses, Jason realized that the "owners" of this group had their "workers" attention. The researchers rarely or never left this place and work took place at all hours.

"I guess if you are really interested in something, its not really work. These people were really dedicated, left their homes across the sea, settled in a new world and learned its language to name but a few obstacles they had to overcome."

Many other streams of thought went through Jason's mind, but all were trumped upon the site of a cafeteria. He quickly ascended the steps to the main door, then walked in. Finding the hostess, he was soon seated. The menu was presented and considering how hungry he was, all items looked good. Selecting one when the waitress came about, he waited while the food was prepared. Within a few minutes he found himself day dreaming again, this time about whether or not the original scientists and engineers has come to this exact place, sat in these seats and talked of turbo pumps and propellants. He wondered also what was in store for him.

The food came, was eaten and then paid for. Jason arose to address the evening, as the sun had gone down by now. He walked outside, looked around for a different route home, decided on the original route and started to go back to his apartment. The other inhabitants outside were alone and quiet; he wondered what other projects were going on that required these 'need to know' people.

111

After entering his new "palace," he turned on the TV only to find out that it was made up of pretty innocuous content. History, military and local news, no HBO. He turned it off, looked at the clock and decided to read in bed until he fell asleep. He checked over his notes, read a good portion of a book on the local history, conveniently placed in his room, and started to fall asleep.

Upon the edge of a dream, Jason turned over and went to sleep. The dream, intense enough to wake him up, had something to do with listening to static on a short wave radio. Listening for far away lands with low power transmitters, talking of rebel invasion or criticizing the politics of a neighboring country. Jason fell back asleep until the morning.

He arose before seven, got prepared for the day and went downstairs to locate the shuttle. I appeared at 20 minute intervals, the next one of which would get him to the conference room well before nine. He looked for a paper to read before his bus trip but found none.

"Par for the course," he thought.

He gathered his back pack, walked to the bus when it arrived and took the short ride to the conference center. His badge was already out, as most of the people on the bus had theirs out. Few people spoke, but he noticed an attractive young women, who he thought was named Christine, based on a glimpse of her badge. The color of her badge was different than Jason's, he knew that that had meaning of some sort. At the stop nearest the conference center, he looked quickly at the girl as he walked down the center isle, trying to make eye contact but failing to do so and simply left the bus and walked to the main entrance. Maybe he would see her later, after work.

In the main lobby he found Susan.

"Good morning."

"Good morning. Are your accommodation adequate?"

"Oh, they're fine, as long as I don't have to stay there for the rest of my life."

Jason smiled saying this, Susan smirked.

She continued, "there have been some major developments, we need to get you to the conference room quickly."

She led him to the first security card operated door, stopped and motioning him through, made sure he was on his way before she left.

Jason wondered about the developments. Wondered if there was a resolution to the main burning questions.

113

He took the elevator to the third floor, then over the to the conference room as he had the day before. Although he was early for the meeting, most of the people who were there yesterday were already present. Coffee was out, voices low and as Jason took his seat, someone closed the doors. Jason was disappointed in this because the avenue of escape was now cut off.

Leslie appeared and looked like she might have been up all night. Before she sat down she addressed the members in the room.

"We have......please close that other door.....ok, we have significant developments on the Pulsar beacon research. Last night and early this morning we received a series of reports from *Gaea*. The first report acknowledged our concerns about the nature of the beacon and confirmed the details of its origin and composition. The second report discusses details of their high power beam and confirms that they have indeed blown off the atmospheres of, as it turns out, many inhabited planets. The immense power of the directed pulsar radiation is used, sometimes at full force, to essentially restart the compete ecosystem of a planet. It appears that the civilization that has employed the power of these pulsars, either singly or in conjunction with other sets of pulsars, is firing this weapon at planets who have

114

developed enough industry and technology to pollute their atmospheres and poison their lands. The degree of destruction has to be very high, where little or no effort has been exercised to clean up or contain the development of the harmful technologies. These planets have selfishly traded their environment, including flora and fauna, for a temporary increase the living standard of a small portion of the population."

Leslie paused to catch her breath.

Jason, raised his hand a bit and asked:

"Excuse me Leslie, but how did the engineers of *Gaea* get so much detailed information about the...for lack of a better term, Pulsar civilization?"

"Because they are in two way communication with that civilization."

"Wow!"

Leslie continued, "and that brings me to the details of the third report, received just an hour ago. The pulsar civilization (she looked at Jason when she said this) is asking questions. Questions about our technology and especially our nuclear technology. They want to know how many weapons we have exploded, how many weapons we have stockpiled, how many nuclear power plants we have in operation and whether or not we have produced a black

115

hole."

Leslie let these words sink in to the assembled scientists and engineers. There was silence for about twenty seconds, then:

"What does the President think?"

"The White House is considering this development. Other agencies, for instance the military, are considering these details as well. As you know, there are well over 10,000 nuclear devices in this world, a significant amount of them are in the megaton class. The President on the one hand wants to avoid any problems with the Pulsar civilization but on the other hand, does not want to divulge the amount and power of the weapons we and our allies have."

"What if we tell them we have none and are purely a peaceful civilization?"

"Well," answered Leslie, "that brings me to the final part of the third message, which is that they have dispatched a probe to our solar system and will compare our answers to their tests. These tests as you can imagine will be comprehensive and accurate. This is a very advanced people, hiding these nuclear devices will probably be futile. And by the way, hiding the scars left in our soil, water and atmosphere will be impossible."

116

"When will the probe arrive?"

"Assuming it can go near the speed of light, 21 years. However between now and then we have to answer their questions, obviously they have the power to point the pulsar radiation towards us, they can't retrieve the energy once its started. The people on *Gaea,* because they are so much closer, are formulating the answer right now, hope they get it right."

Leslie stopped for a moment, she looked exhausted and worried. She continued:

"I'm tired so we are going to break up for now, we need to re-convene here every day to review the reports, formulate an opinion and send that opinion to Washington. For the next many years we will in essence be sequestered, absolutely no discussions about this issue leaves this room. Security as you know it will be enhanced significantly."

Jason was not happy to hear this, security to him was already oppressive, now it will be more so.

"Tomorrow," was Leslie's parting word.

The assembled people rose and filed to the door, most feeling like this was going to be a prison of sorts for the next several years. Jason waited a bit and when able asked Leslie:

"Do I have an office here?"

117

"Yes, see Susan about that and anything else you need."

She then left, Jason was the last, but before he exited, he walked over to the window and opened the shades, looked out and realized he was on his own small planet now. After a moment, he went downstairs to the main lobby, found Susan there, on a cell phone and waited until she was done.

"Sorry I was talking to Leslie, I guess there have been some changes."

"Yeah, I think so."

"Well, we have an office for you on the forth floor, and apparently will be moving you yet again into a larger apartment, maybe even a house."

Her demeanor was much softer now, she obviously had been told by Leslie that Jason's world was now permanently changed and that he would now endure permanent restrictions.

"Where exactly is my office?"

"Forth floor, office 425, about in the middle."

"Window?"

"Two, in fact...its nice."

"Can I check it out now?"

"Of course, make a list of what you want in there,

118

even new furniture, think of yourself as a special guest. In fact, all of your expenses will be taken care of."

Jason sighed, "Ok, thanks, I'm going to check out my office and start writing a report, see you later?"

"Yes, and here is my cell number, contact me 24/7 for anything you need."

"Thank you."

Jason left Susan in the lobby, went upstairs to check out his new office and on the way there passed several people in the hallway. He thought about whether or not they knew what was going on.

At his new office, he opened the door, went inside and looked around; not bad, decent computer, double monitor, nice windows.

"Just where I want to spend the next twenty years." he smirked.

He stayed there for a few hours, getting to know the limits of his access on the computer. He also re-arranged his furniture and fully opened the window shades. As it was getting near noon, and he was basically done for the day, he decided to leave.

"Not like they're going to fire me."

He made it out a side door, scrutinized by several cameras and access devices. Across the lawn to the

119

shuttle stop. He waited for several minutes, a bus came and getting on board, he was happily surprised to see the same attractive girl that was on the morning bus.

"Hello."

"Hello."

After a few more pleasantries, they found themselves talking in earnest. She was an engineer working on a special project. Jason knew not to ask further considering the clearance level and his sense of being watched. He did not go into detail regarding his activities but implied he was going to be here for a while. At one point in the conversation, they joked about not being able to tell each other the details of their work. Christine looked a Jason and just for fun said:

"Actually, I am an alien, sent from a far away star to find out if the human race has been behaving."

Jason froze.

"What.... what I say?"

~The Voyages of Gaea~

BENTHIC 2

"No matter where you go - there you are"
- Confucius

121

"We've decided not to explore this world but instead fly to within a few billion miles to get a decent visual and infrared analysis," the management team of *Gaea* announced over the intranet. "It is our opinion that there are greater opportunities in the next star system and considering its distance, we should not stop and explore what looks like a life marginal planet.

Rudy was crushed. To himself he said:

"I just spent nearly a year studying this planet, gave up a dozen other opportunities for in situ research and now this. What a waste, this is horrible."

He paced around in his office/lab frustrated by the seemingly simple decision that erased a year of intense effort. His blood pressure was up and its manifestations scared a co-worker when she walked in.

His friend and confidant, Laurie Espinosa saw him, walked over and said, "Goodness, your face is beet red. What is the matter, are you ok?"

"Fine, just fine. I've just received word that we are not stopping at Benthic 2, its going to take too much time they say. Rats!"

"Well, calm down, in fact sit down, I insist. It's not the end of the world, your research will still be very useful. A future mission I'm sure will read your work and it will be immensely helpful to them."

"It *is* the end of the world. I don't know what is going to happen in the future, probably nothing the way things are going, we certainly won't return this way when we decide to go back to Earth. This world has the most unique ecological and geological signatures I have ever seen. They are upset that there isn't strong evidence of an advanced culture. Who cares? Who cares if they're just bugs and fish, there is so much to learn by going there. This place looks beautiful and serene, we should go there for no other reason than a vacation."

"We can't afford a vacation Rudy, you know, we are behind schedule. Management is worried about not getting home in time for many of the younger crew members to see Earth again, and that's in our charter."

"They should have thought about that when we spent so many weeks at L'quacious 5. And that stupid diversion for the Pulsar civilization, we didn't need that either."

"Of course we needed to divert, any mistakes with that encounter could have cost massive destruction on Earth. You know that."

"Yeah, well, I'm still upset."

"I can see that. And remember, I spent almost a

123

year in research as well. It's not just your problem. Let's consider where we are and what options we have. We and especially you know more details about this world than anyone on this ship. Maybe we should consider some alternative approaches to complete our mission. We should consider sending a probe, and its a forgone conclusion that we will get the majority of the time on the biggest astronomical instruments on board during our flyby."

"Its not the same as going there, we can learn so much from this world, it has the most unique signatures, it must be a paradise down there." Rudy was calming down, especially with the smoothing influence of his research partner, Laurie.

"You're probably right, but these are the options we have now."

"Hmmm, send a probe? That certainly would be useful, but again, not the same as being there, smelling the fresh air (which this place has a lot of) or seeing its oceans, which by our sensors are very deep and apparently crystal clear. It would be like going to the Bahamas, Laurie. Can you imagine going underwater and being able to see twenty miles?" He looked up at her at this last proclamation.

"Sounds wonderful, Rudy, however what other options do we have?"

Rudy hesitated for a moment, turned to his laptop computer, typed in some questions to the ship wide search engine. In a few seconds he turned back to Laurie.

"They now have a spare shuttle."

Laurie though for a second, "Rudy, that would be an enormous and dangerous journey. The shuttles are too small for more than one person and the food requirements. The flight would be more than four months there and then at least six more to get back to *Gaea* because we would have moved away from the star system. You'd go nuts."

"People have been isolated for years and made it. You know, marooned sailors on South Pacific islands..."

"Sure, but they did not have to contend with only 100 cubic meters of space. And especially with all kinds of equipment on board, just to keep you alive; its a huge risk."

"Oh come on, its very relaxing out there, I could read 100's of books, and if I get claustrophobic, I'll just go for a walk."

"Very funny. Remember to put out the trash. Oh and by the way, all you have to do is get your hair brained scheme past a few dozen review boards."

"I am willing to try."

"Well then, go for it Robinson Crusoe."

Rudy went back to his office. He knew he had

125

some leverage insofar as he was one of the few experts on this world, it looked very inviting which gave the management board pause in the decision. So there was an interest in exploring it, now the trick would be convince the board he should do this solo. The best approach would be to write a proposal and pass it by his peers for comment. After any required polishing he could go to the next level. Then if he was lucky, training, and launch. He had, by his estimation, about two months to make this all happen.

He got to work that evening, collating all of his research on Benthic 2, he made a master outline, executive summary, lists of required equipment and supplies, a detailed description of the science to be performed and a schedule. It took several days to accomplish the writing but ultimately it looked good and detailed enough to make his peers take it seriously. Rudy bound it with a clear cover, made sure the pictures and diagrams looked appealing and made twenty copies.

"Looks good, I made some redlines, but in general I like it," was his first response from a reviewer.

"The risk appears to be addressed and minimized, I would, if I were you, highlight the scientific rewards from such an expedition," was the second response.

Others followed, from which he made a final

126

proposal and after a review from Laurie, he held his breath and sent it to the management review panel that ultimately would have to make a recommendation to the chief executive.

The hours rolled by slowly and eventually turned into days. The wait could be interpreted as either a serious attempt to understand the proposal or they were simply busy and had little time to look at it.

After an arduous wait, he received a response from the panel, it read:

"Proposal received, under review, need:

1. Detailed summary of flight experience.
2. Complete medical records
3. Psychological evaluation"

"This I think is good news," Rudy thought.

He gathered his log books, contacted his physician and arranged for a psych eval. Rudy had extensive flight experience, from piston, through jet to hybrid aircraft. He had experience with marginal weather, instrument flight and had a penchant for good decision making while flying.

He responded to the panel with what information he

had as well as alerting them as to the schedule with the psychologist. He had to move quickly to keep their attention as well as not miss an opportunity to gain valuable experience.

Within 24 hours, his flight logs and medical records were being evaluated, the psych review was set for the next day, but this caused Rudy a bit of concern. What questions would be asked, what was the right approach to talking to the psychologist? His answers would come soon enough.

At the appointed time, Rudy made his way to the human factors center on the ship. He waited for a bit in a comfortable lobby, wondering what would happen next, then a door opened with a person inviting him in to the office. Once inside, he noticed over stuffed chairs and sofas, along with a desk. The objects in the room were nondescript, nothing particularly interesting. The psychologist looked up from her notes.

"Good morning, I'm Dr. Michelle Friedman, please sit down."

Rudy sat down, looked around a bit and waited.

"Would you like some coffee?"

"No, thanks."

A pregnant silence followed, then Rudy spoke again.

"So....you going to ask if I love my mother?"

"Oh I hope we don't end up there," was the response, "I just have some simple questions, no big deal."

He paused a bit more.

"I was just interested in why you want to make this trip," she asked as she put down her papers and adjusted herself to a more comfortable position.

While she looked at him with an open, un-blinking manner, he said:

"Oh....Well I just realized that this was a wonderful opportunity that should not be ignored. I understand the decisions of the management council to forego a complete exploratory mission, not upset by it but more concerned with the loss of a potential wealth of knowledge. I think that a reduced magnitude mission can be accomplished with little risk and significant amount of gain."

He waited for a response, which was:

"Hmmm," that was it for a long moment. She continued, "Well I can see that you're motivated, maybe for good reason, but tell me what potential risks you see as easy to overcome."

"Well of course there will be plenty of food, so no problems there, then there will be the things to do over the long trip. Just the science alone will keep me very busy,

129

then....."

"I understand you might be in a small confined area for up to six months, are you aware that in many experiments in the past, that kind of isolation can lead to psychotic episodes?"

"I have read a bit about that, and I think its a matter of discipline."

"Discipline?"

"During the daily ritual, having things that need to be done becomes very important. Having a focus on tasks, and in a way I won't be completely alone, I will be communicating with *Gaea* on a daily basis, maybe even you," he smiled when he said this, she did not.

"Oh believe me we will talk often if you are allowed to go."

"And the motivation for this will help me to focus. In other words, the knowledge that we will gain upon landing on this world and the wealth of discoveries that would be waiting would keep me in a positive mood so to speak."

"And if there is nothing there? Or dangers that you did not anticipate?"

"As I get closer, I will know more and more about this world, the instruments will be more and more in focus every day that goes by. I'll have many chances to abort the mission if I or we see a problem."

"Ok, um, let me ask you a hypothetical question....if Einstein had discovered after decades of work, that his theories in general relativity had major insurmountable problems and that he had, during the course of his working life, defended his work vigorously to the point of vilifying and humiliating his critics, how would he feel at that point?"

"Embarrassed."

"Anything more?"

"Well I guess, angry."

"How angry?"

"Extremely, he had worked so long on this project, had humiliated his detractors and now he had nothing. I would guess very, very angry."

"And do you think at the point of his greatest anger, he should make decisions that could effect his life?"

"No, absolutely not, that would be dangerous."

"Exactly," she stopped, sat back in her chair, and waited for the light to go off in Rudy's head.

"Well, that's not going to happen to me."

"Sure it could, you could have an on-board emergency, you could find hidden dangers on the surface of the planet, lots of possibilities," she leaned forward now and placed her head on her hands while her elbows resting on the desk in front of her. She waited again."

"Then we need checks and balances."

"How so?"

"Periodic evaluations of my mental state, periodic evaluations of the progress of the mission."

"Anything else?"

Rudy thought for a while and sensing the go/no go nature of this meeting, knew what he had to say.

"And a fail safe option, like taking over the flight computer remotely."

"And what about your father?"

"My father?"

"Do you love your father?"

"He's gone now, but yes I did."

"More than your mother?"

"Well, I just......"

"Ok, you can go now," she interrupted, "I will have my report complete by tomorrow, do you have a questions for me?"

Rudy felt like he was standing on razor blades. "No, not now, thank you for your time."

She looked up, smiled warmly, held out her hand and said:

"Thank you for coming in, good luck."

"Of course, thank you as well."

Rudy left the room quickly, "now what did all of that mean?" Was it positive, was it an indication of their major concerns about the mission? Why did she lean back in her chair an look at me that way? What's with the stupid pictures on the wall?

"Sometimes a cigar is just a cigar," Rudy's friend told him upon hearing the details of the interview that evening. "Freud said that, in other words don't over-interpret. Things will be as things will be, if there is a good reason why you should not go, then even you will understand and agree. And of course if there are no problems, then you should feel assured that the professionals realize that you are in good enough mental shape to accomplish your mission. Many years ago, at NASA, the flight physicians would tell the astronaut applicants that is was their job to keep them out of the corp, in other words look for any problem whatsoever and wash them out, once they were accepted however, into the ranks of the astronauts, it was their job to keep them in the corp. Keep that in mind."

"Thanks, I will."

Surprisingly, at least in Rudy's mind, he was given the okay from the psychologist. Next stop was the flight department. Although Rudy had significant experience with single and multi-engine aircraft, even some experience with tilt-rotors, he was no match to the professional pilots in the flight department. They flew the shuttles on a daily basis, either to planets they were in orbit around or on inspection tours of the large spacecraft itself. Each had thousands of hours in hundreds of air and spacecraft.

The next morning, he walked into the flight ready room, which already had several pilots in it, some in their "fast pants." Rudy looked around, found a seat near the middle of a table and sat down. Within a few minutes, the room was mostly full. Interestingly, the seat directly across the table from Rudy was left open until the last person filed in. He was in his 50s, flight suit on, multiple patches, including jet, rocket, space station and top gun. He was holding a large file of papers and a map. Sitting down, he looked up at Rudy.

"Rudy, I'm Colonel Young, let's get down to business."

Everyone in the room quieted down and waited for the colonel to continue.

"Ok, lets see, 1st class medical, psych test okay, 2,500 hours flight time, no incidents, accidents. Single, Multi, Tilt, glider, taildragger....I like that one, a little bit of space sim.......okay (he looked up at Rudy), here's the deal: Before we can sign you off, we need a lot of ground school, a lot of sim time and three instructors need to endorse you. After all of that I fly with you for a final check ride."

He looked pensive for a moment, flipped back and forth with some papers, put his finger on some page inside the folder, then, closing the folder, looked up.

"Son, this won't be easy, and I don't mean the flying part. You are going to spend a lot of time alone in a sophisticated shuttle. There are numerous and I mean numerous systems which you have to babysit on a daily basis. You start going mental on us we're going to pull the plug. We have full Mode R authority on this mission. You drift off into la-la land and we will disable your flight director and bring you home. The training you will receive will be tough, and I mean mentally tough, we aim to break you son, we need to know where that point is and if you have the character to recognize that point and adjust accordingly. The instructors are going to watch you closely and drill into that brain of yours to find out what you're made of. We are going to yank you and bank you, make you hit the limits, your going inside, outside and inverted, then we are going to do some real flying."

The Colonel paused for a moment, Rudy smiled at

the last statement, no one else did. Rudy un-smiled quickly.

"First up is ground school 0700 tomorrow, Major Dagle is going to give you the flight manuals, study up and study up hard. If you make it through his course, then we will start teaching you how to fly."

Rudy thought about saying "I can fly, and I can fly well," but in this case discretion was the better part of valor.

"Any questions," from the Colonel.

"No, sir."

"Alright, dismissed."

Everyone rose, and standing in place, waited for the Colonel to depart. After that, they looked a Rudy, made some internal judgements, and left the room. Major Dagle remained, walked over to a table by the wall, pickup up the first foot of three feet of flight manuals, gave it to Rudy and said:

"Get through these for tomorrow, see you at 0700."

"Roger that."

Rudy ran back to the apartment, closed the shades, cleaned off the dining room table and started with the first volume. The shuttle had systems in many ways similar to a jet aircraft, this of course was done to aid transition of a jet pilot to a spacecraft pilot. The primary and secondary instruments were in the same places. There where

136

however significant changes in the navigation and power plant systems. Rudy studied these in detail, discovering primary, secondary and tertiary systems for every major component of the spacecraft. He took notes as he went and made a cheat sheet of the most important thrust setting, speeds, and control attributes; these he would have to commit to memory. He studied until 1 a.m. Then decided that he should go to sleep in anticipation of a long day.

That day came quickly, as he arose and dealt with the lack of sleep, excitement and absolute need to get to class on time. Running in the apartment, he, with minutes to spare, finished his chores and made it out the front door. He ran down the hallways to the main spine "avenue" then ran the rest of the way to the classroom. Ten minutes early, he fell in the door and found his instructor waiting for him, with several projectors displaying major system block diagrams. He sat down, adjusted his paperwork and just as he found a writing implement class started.

They spent the next four hours on the attributes of thrust, navigation, human factors and emergency procedures. The general teaching method was presentation, questions about the details then Rudy had to teach the instructor about the details. This method was exhausting but effective. Rudy had lunch in the classroom

137

then had another four hours of ground school. After a full day, the instructor turned off his projectors and laptops and sat down near Rudy in a more relaxed manner. The instructor's intent was to find you who his student really was.

"Long day, huh," was the instructor's opening.

"Yeah, there are a lot of details, many I need to memorize."

"Have any further questions?"

"Oh, about three hundred, my brains full right now, so tonight I am going to write down the major ones and ask them tomorrow. I do have one question however, before I go back to the cabin."

"Shoot."

"What's it like to fly this contraption?" Rudy smiled at his own question, the instructor did not.

"It like flying a 747-800 and an F-22 at the same time; elegant and smooth going slow, but very closely coupled going fast. Get behind this spacecraft and your in real trouble. Hope your skills are sharp."

"I look forward to the sim."

"Good, but we have to get through the ground school first. Tomorrow, book two, special and emergency procedures, study up."

138

"Roger that."

Rudy and the instructor rose, gathered their belongings and departed. Rudy went back to his cabin for dinner and a night of book work. So far the only scary thing was the amount of details which he needed to commit to memory. Before his simulator ride he would have to understand the limits and procedures necessary to fly the shuttle safely. But he knew that would only be a start, just like real world pilots, the sim rides would not be standard, but filled with emergencies, malfunctions, system failures and general heart pounding excitement. What he did not know was that the simulators he would eventually fly also had realistic noise, smoke and movement that would required full aerobatic seat belts.

He studied hard that night, until midnight. More notes, cheat sheets and questions. He would show up earlier the next morning to get additional time with the instructor.

Again, morning came quickly, he was out of the apartment in record time, showing up thirty minutes early. The instructor was already there and said:

"Showing some incentive I see....good."

That day again was spent on the manuals but finished up sitting on a folding chair in front of cardboard

139

cutouts of the instrument panels on the shuttle. After studying the systems for several days, it was now time to commit their positions to muscle memory. Rudy sat in the seat with his eyes closed and pointed at the appropriate knob or switch when the instructor called out a control function. This game went on for several hours but gave Rudy a very good sense of where to go quickly if something went wrong.

The last day of ground school was spent with written, oral and practical (using the cutouts) tests. Rudy, exhausted, finished and passed with a decent grade.

"Go over your emergency procedures many times before you get into the sim," advised the instructor.

"Oh, absolutely."

"No, I mean really go over every scenario, be prepared for things to go bad right after launch, multiple systems, lots of distractions. Remember, there will come a time when you have to prioritize several problems during an emergency. Think about what you need most when that happens."

"Got it, I'll start reviewing this immediately."

"Good, cause your in sim day after tomorrow."

"Thanks, I appreciate your helping me."

"No problem, and good luck, just remember that

when the flight instructor gets quiet, something is about to happen.

"Ok."

Rudy went back to his cabin, exhausted from the book work and tests, opened a beer and sat down to go over the emergency section of the flight manuals again. He had dinner, worked some more and went to sleep early that evening.

Within a few days, it was time for the sim. He was a bit anxious about this as the sim was a full motion contraption with several operators in a control room. The inside of the sim was as realistic as possible. This included full motion, detailed imagery in all windows, several g's of motion control, smoke, sound, leaks and all realistic controls and instruments. But most imposing was the instructor, a veteran of thousands of hours of flight time in the line shuttles. He had experienced the emergencies, all of the flight scenarios and had been the first pilot to land on another star's planet. His name was Ben, in his 50's and although friendly, had a very serious streak in him when conditions called for it. No nonsense during all phases of flight. If you were serious about flying then you would be serious when flying with him.

Sim day one, Rudy climbed the stairs into the sim

141

cockpit.

"Close the door and lock it," came the voice from the darkened interior.

Rudy did as he was told and as his eyes adjusted to the darkness he began to make out instrument lights, displays and two people inside. Ben was in the right seat and another instructor who sat at a control panel in the back of the cockpit.

"Take your seat."

Rudy went to the captain's side of the cockpit and sat down, strapped in his five point harness and viewed the cockpit layout. The second instructor rose, threw a switch labeled "Full motion," sat down and strapped in as well. The cockpit was more definable now, all of the instruments were placed where the manuals had said, the controls were worn from use. Rudy felt comfortable.

"Ok, lets get the engines started," Ben said.

"Pre-start checklist complete?"

"A firm."

"Ok, fuel pumps on, hydraulics on, electricals to main bus A." Rudy knew most of this by heart as he went through the checklist, going directly to the place on the control panels for each function he needed to address. He was thankful now for the cardboard cutout training.

142

"Engine one starter engage, thirty percent N1, fuel flow on, watch for hot start."

The engines were powered by a Hydrogen and Oxygen combination which gave a very controllable output thrust.

He started all four engines, pressurized the hull, started the avionics and programmed the flight management system. As he did this the displays switched to a very detailed view of the launch bay. This view was complete with people moving about, other moving machinery and sounds.

"Wow!"

"Lets keep focused."

Rudy went back to work, securing all necessary systems, completing all checklists, only then did he look up to view the "outside world."

Ben started, "Establish communications, open your flight plan and prepare for takeoff."

Rudy smiled, adjusted his microphone and headset.

"Ground control, shuttle five is at position nine, ready for shuttle bay taxi, we have information Alpha."

One of the control room personnel replied:

"Shuttle five, good morning, taxi to launch position one via taxiway Bravo, give way to personnel and

143

equipment on the ramp."

"Shuttle five to launch position one, Bravo, give way to personnel and equipment."

Now the hard part, the engines needed to remain at idle, but vectored downward to allow the shuttle to start moving forward. Too much angle and it would lift off vertically (as this was in 1/3 gravity), too little angle and nothing would happen. His lack of experience would show here, but careful use of the flight controls enabled him to carefully start the craft moving.

After a five minute taxi through and around obstacles in the launch bay:

"Shuttle five at launch position one, ready for takeoff."

"Shuttle five, departure control, cleared for take off, turn right, heading 030 by plus 15, do not exceed 100 kph, contact traffic control on 2138.75."

"Cleared for take off, right turn 030 by plus 15, not to exceed 100 kph and 2138.75 for traffic control, Shuttle five."

With that, Rudy advanced the throttles a bit to start moving, adjusting the collective (engine angle controls) to gain altitude and moved through the main launch bay doors which had been opened during the radio transmissions. He felt the tilting of the craft and the sense of acceleration as he moved through the opening. So far so good, but he knew to remain vigilant. The departure took them into the starry night, the view out of the right window clearly showed the starboard side of the great ship. Rudy for the first time finally realized how incredibly large this spacecraft was, it went on for literally many kilometers. The details were amazing, and that was the last of the site-seeing.

"Shuttle five, traffic control, we have radar contact and show you off course, turn left twenty degrees, traffic at twelve o'clock, two kilometers, robotic vessel, no lights."

"Roger, turning left twenty, looking for traffic."

Twelve red lights illuminated on the control panel, warning buzzers went off and the flight management computer started giving alerts.

"Traffic alert, traffic alert, descend, descend! Engine three fire warning! Pressurization alert!"

Rudy very quickly pushed the nose of the shuttle over, lifting the three crew members out of their seats, at the same time he reached over and pulled the number two fire extinguisher button out, then he started to fumble with the pressurization controls, not sure what the problem was.

"Ok," said Ben, "lets reset."

Rudy was sweating at this point even though

145

everything was going well up until the last few minutes. His heart was pounding.

"Ok, relax," Ben advised, "you need to be very cool under these conditions, very cool, in fact, next time this happens, push the autopilot on and wind the clock."

"What? Wind the clock?"

"No one has ever been killed when the pilot wound the clock, but going too fast in the cockpit has done it many, many times. First, the robotic ship was on your radar, and was two minutes flight time away, always look at your radar first to confirm. Next look at the pressurization, the secondary system had already taken over and corrected the problem. Last, you were moving so fast that you extinguished the fire in number two, which was not on fire, and left number three to burn. Luckily the automatic systems took control or we would have just exploded."

"Yeah, ok, how about another run."

"Gladly." He pressed the push to talk button on the control column. "Ground, lets reset the scenario, and this time, don't be so nice."

"Roger that, sim. Push all the buttons."

Rudy was not exactly glad to hear this conversation but knew he could handle it, he just needed to relax and use his skills as a pilot.

The sim reset to inside the hangar, just ready for takeoff. The instructor instinctively cinched up his belt, Rudy saw this and did the same.

Rudy thought, "Cool, just be cool, remember Bob Hoover, Chuck Yeager and Neil Armstrong."

Again, he went through the checklist, but at a slightly slower pace, just to make sure nothing was missed. Again, he lifted off, moved toward the launch bay opening and exited the spacecraft. Within 30 seconds, there was a fire warning in the avionics bay, Rudy calmly changed the power bus to the emergency setting and engaged the fire extinguishing system. Then the flight controller announced large amounts of stellar debris (small meteorites up to ten feet in diameter) in the vicinity of the flight path, moving very quickly. Rudy adjusted the radar display for maximum range to start tracking. All this while maintaining a precise flight path around the large spaceship, doing an inspection patrol. Other emergencies appeared, loss of pressurization, loss of electricals, fuel problems, flight director problems, autopilot disconnects. This time they were methodically taken care of and a safe flight was executed.

After what seemed like minutes in one way and hours in another, he returned to sim to the launch bay and performed a nice landing.

147

"How was that, chief?"

"Reasonable, we'll talk it over in the de-brief room."

They both exited the sim and although tired went into a room covered with posters depicting system block diagrams and large graphs showing performance curves for various space vehicles. They sat down, were given water and the instructor went into a detailed analysis of each maneuver and emergency. Methodically, they reviewed and graded each task and talked about alternative approaches if necessary. After another hour of discussion, they planned the next day's activities and Rudy was dismissed.

He went directly to his quarters and collapsed. After an hour's nap, he awoke, opened the books again, ate dinner and prepared for the next day.

The next day went a bit smoother than the previous, followed by three more days of sim, culminating in a check ride by the Chief pilot.

The check ride was a review of the major emergencies practiced on the days before. By this time however, Rudy was experienced and maintained perfect control of the machine. One maneuver after another, he expertly prioritized the problems and took care of them, one by one.

148

"Not bad," is all he got from the Check pilot as he endorsed Rudy's logbook and signed him off for the mission.

Then the pilot looked up at Rudy and said, "now the hard part." He put his pen down, sat back in his chair and studying Rudy for a moment said, "flying this machine is only the tip of the iceberg as far as this mission is concerned. Actually, the next signoff comes from you, you must make the decision to make this journey. I don't have to tell you that this trip of yours is really going to be a mental exercise. You have the skills to fly the shuttle, no doubt, but the hard part is going to be keeping the discipline necessary for a long, solo mission like this. The discipline to keep the shuttle in perfect shape. Take care of it and it will take care of you. Who knows were your mind is going to lead you on those long and lonely days while en route to the planet. Remember Lindberg? He sat in the cockpit for almost two days never letting go of the controls, at one point he calculated the number of times the cylinders had moved up and down during the flight, he almost fell asleep a couple of times as well, but he kept his eye on the prize at all times and made it across the Atlantic. And if I were to show you the aircraft he flew for 38 hours across the Atlantic Ocean in, you would tell me that it was impossible. The thing was tiny, in fact it had no windshield, he used a periscope for take off and landing...

"I've seen it, at the Ford museum," interrupted Rudy.

"See how small it was?" asked the senior pilot.

"Yes, it was tiny."

"Well that is how small the shuttle is going to feel after a few months in space. Make absolutely sure you are mentally prepared for this."

The pilot leaned forward, looked at Rudy with 20,000 hours of cumulative flight time eyes.

"Report to me here at 0900 tomorrow morning with your decision."

"Aye, sir."

The Chief pilot rose and looked at the wall clock, then at Rudy. He then turned and exited the classroom. Rudy sat for a moment, reflecting on the week's activities, then reflected on the chief pilot's comments. After what seemed to be twenty minutes, he rose and left to return to his quarters. His thoughts on his way back were mostly on his motivations with a smattering of proud as he had passed several rigorous tests both as a pilot and as psychologically qualified to make this journey.

Once at his quarters, he walked in, put down his manuals, walked to the refrigerator, pulled out a beer and opening it, sat down to consider his situation. He was exhausted but happy and came to realize that his motivations about this journey were part of his being. To stay back was not an option.

A second beer followed the first, and at some point after a few sips, Rudy realized he was exhausted. He sat back in his chair and for fun, closed his eyes and pointed to the systems and switches in the cockpit he had memorized in the simulator and shuttles. He smiled at the fact that he had learned most of these details in the paper cockpit, sitting on a folding chair.

"What a useful tool," he thought.

Soon, the exhaustion overtook him and he went to bed, cognizant of the fact that he needed to talk intelligently in the morning. He drank a large glass of water and took some aspirin.

Falling asleep quickly, Rudy remained almost motionless in his sleep. He dreamt of flying in space, of having emergencies and of landing on a foreign planet.

The next morning, he awoke somewhat refreshed, maybe a "schooling" hangover if anything. He ate well, had some tea and a good shower. Dressing in decent clothes, he prepared for his last hurdle. Taking a deep breath before he opened the door to the hallway of his living area, he

151

reached over, took the handle, wished himself good luck and started his walk to the conference room.

Down the pristine halls, filled with people, voices, the hum of air transport machinery and the smell of clean floors. Cleaning was done at "night," so the mornings gave the crew members fresh hallways and work space. By the evening the effects of use were evident.

Rudy turned left onto the main hallway or promenade, continued for several hundred feet, turned right into the hallway where the flight ops resided. He found the door to the conference room he had spent so many hours in over the last few weeks, walked in, and found himself looking at the chief pilot, chief psychologist, manager of *Gaea* operations, several shuttle pilots, and a few of his friends. He was taken aback by the number and caliber of the people inside the room and as a result, hesitated as he entered the room. Feeling embarrassed or nervous, his confidence waned for a moment, but returned as he felt solid in his conviction that this was the right course of action.

"Please sit down."

"Thank you, hello to everyone," Rudy said, looking primarily at his friends. They nodded in greeting. Everyone sat down.

The chief pilot started the conversation:

"Welcome back, its been a while (he smiled for once), you did nicely on your check ride, your paperwork is in order and sign-offs complete. The people in this room have no objections to you taking this journey and have educated you as to the risks and challenges you will face. You have passed *our* tests but we would like to know how you are feeling about this and if you have had any second thoughts?"

"No, I do not," started Rudy. "I have actually enjoyed the challenge of talking, working and learning from the people assembled in this room. I initially thought I would have to write down a response, thinking carefully about the impact of my words and being concerned about saying the wrong thing that would jeopardize my chances of walking down that hall (he raised his hands and pointed towards the launch bay), but really, that is not the case. Walking out of my room this morning and down the halls, coming here to see my colleagues and friends, made me feel good, inspired and confirmed my dedication to performing a flawless, professional journey to this planet. When I first asked for this mission, it was due to my concern that we would miss an important opportunity to explore what appears to be a fascinating, rich world, most likely with life

153

of some sort on it. The observations indicate much will be learned by the exploration of this world. It is however one of many opportunities which we have considered and it came in "second" in terms of the amount of effort and resources required to move our great ship from its present heading to go into orbit around the planet. A smaller mission, however is acceptable and if done properly will give our researchers more options to learn as we travel through space as we have over the last several years. My motivation is not only professional but for a lack of a better word, social. The information we will garner will be substantial during this voyage but I have to admit that there is another more personal reason why I want to go Benthic 2. To some degree, there are not words that describe my motivation, and this is because those words were not needed for the many explorers that proceeded me over the history of our people. Something in our souls motivates us to explore, to look past the next hill, mountain, ocean or planetary system. It somehow is built in and is one of the reasons for our success as a people. I am just responding to this motivation and have had the good luck and fortune to be here to continue the work."

"Although I agree about your motivation, I think luck and fortune are only a minor contributor. Your skills and knowledge have led you here and we, as the members of the greater community are lucky to have you represent us in this mission." the operations manager said.

"Thank you, I will do my best."

The chief pilot looked up, straight faced, "You're right about that."

With that, the attendees rose to shake Rudy's hand and wish him luck. Rudy went around the room, ending up with his friends to say goodbye. Within a few minutes it was all over, it was then, for the first time, that Rudy realized this was real.

He walked slowly back to his quarters, taking in the view, sounds and smells, gathered his most essential items, and a few personal mementos for the journey. Packing them carefully, he closed up his travel bag, shut off the lights and environmental systems, shut the door to his quarters and walked back to the launch bay. He found a flock of technicians and launch personnel crawling over the shuttle, checking every system, fluid, voltage and adjusting as necessary. QC (Quality Control) personnel followed many of the people, signing off important tests and recording important values. After an hour or so of examination, the personnel finished their duties and made their way back to their offices or labs. Rudy was left alone with the shuttle to do his final inspection and contemplate his fate. He walked around the craft a few times not really paying attention to the details but knowing that it had been checked out thoroughly.

A voice behind him said:

"Ready for this?"

It was the chief pilot, taking a personal interest in the mission.

"Yeah, I think so (emphasis on the 'so')."

"Well, you'll be fine, remember our advice and communicate with us often. We have a mission control center that will be staffed 24 hours a day."

"Thank you."

"Alright then, saddle up, lets get this show on the road."

Rudy looked at his new mentor, shook his hand, and climbed into the shuttle. Turning to his left, he pushed the button that closed the air stairs. Rudy watched the chief pilot until the door was completely shut and sealed. It would be sealed for several months.

Rudy made his way to the cockpit, sat down, put his seat belt and shoulder harness on and got comfortable. After a moment, he reached up and turned on the master switch and proceeded down the pre-flight checklist.

Methodically, he finished up, then started the engine start checklist and opened communications with the launch control operators. He completed each line, verified the operation with the launch personnel and within a few minutes looked up to see the launch bay doors opening to allow him to start the mission.

He adjusted his mike on his headset.

"Launch control, this is Shuttle Aristarchus."

"Aristarchus, launch control, go ahead."

"Shuttle Aristarchus is ready for departure."

"Roger, Aristarchus, you are cleared for departure, turn left to two three zero, plus twenty two. Maintain 100 kph until clear."

"Left two three zero plus twenty two. Maintain 100 kph until clear of *Gaea*."

He advanced the vertical translation control, then tapped the aft thrusters to start the vessel moving toward the door. Soon the launch bay doors were behind him and starting to close and the great ship *Gaea* was receding behind him. Rudy reached over to the flight management computer, engaged it to control the flight director and the shuttle banked to the right and started to accelerate towards his destination.

"Weird," Rudy thought, "nothing bad happened."

He was so used to emergencies in training that it was strange to have nothing happen but normal operations.

After the first hour of flight, he settled in in a more relaxed manner. Communications were frequent with the mother ship. Systems were evaluated as he flew and everything looked "nominal." During the second hour of flight, he felt comfortable enough to unbuckle his seatbelt and move about the cabin. It was like a dream in some ways, floating effortlessly from one end of the shuttle to the other, smooth and quiet. The electronics were working perfectly and as he had discovered, were quite capable of taking care of themselves. Any anomalies would be announced, corrective measures suggested and if there was no response after a short waiting period, autonomous action would be taken to correct the problem.

Another several hours passed, he relaxed, ate a meal and had the first glimmer of boredom. He remembered the advice of the people on *Gaea*, and kept to his routine.

Days past, the visual image of the mother ship was hard to see, even with a telescope. The planet, Benthic 2, could just be discerned in the glare of the star it revolved around. A few months needed to pass before it was clearly in the windshield, with its oceans, forests and mountains.

Using the large telescopes on the mother ship, this planet looked beautiful, rotating on its axis every 20 earth hours. It would be a long voyage but the wait would be worth it.

Meanwhile, *Gaea* changed course and started to accelerate towards a new star system, gliding slowly out of real time communications range. After the first month, messages would come in several hours after they were sent. Any return traffic took the same amount of time.

The daily routines started to deteriorate after six weeks in the shuttle. It felt very small and Rudy had to find unique way to entertain himself. One day he would only consider what used to be the ceiling as the floor, another day it would be a wall. He explored every possible millimeter of the ship, sometimes sleeping near a piece of equipment that had motors in it to remind him of the sounds back home. Day after day, week after week passed, communications with *Gaea* were arduous, people were getting busy there and the excitement of having an away mission faded into the past.

Two months into the journey, Rudy was feeling the stress of confinement and on a few occasions, suited up for an EVA, just to get out of the ship and inspect the exterior, even though several cameras did the same chore with better resolution. He was, however, over the half way point of the journey and on one particular EVA, spend 20 minutes just riding on the top of the shuttle, looking at the slowly enlarging world coming at him.

The EVAs helped, as well as the e-mails from the mother ship. The grind was on, boredom in control of his life. The routine he promised himself and others to follow was cut down to one or two chores a day. Even the EVAs, due to their preparation length, became uninteresting.

On one evening however there was a change. Rudy was sitting in the left hand cockpit chair when, as his eyes were approaching half mast preparing themselves for yet another cat nap, a faint, very faint milky glow appeared to his right. Rudy shifted over to see better, but at first did not take this glow very seriously. Within several minutes however, the glow persisted and Rudy sat up more interested. The glow was like an amorphous cloud suspended between the two pilot seats in the cockpit. It moved laterally every once in a while but for the most part sat suspended in the area above the navigation equipment. Rudy checked the instrumentation but found no anomalies with the exception of a very faint signal on the spectrum analyzer. No alarms yet, if fact is was more fascinating than insidious he felt. He watched for another hour as the shape became a bit more bright and maybe slightly more formed.

160

After several more hours, Rudy started to record images and any other phenomena from his new friend. Rudy ate in its presence, again with the feeling that it was not harmful; much like walking into a room where an old friendly dog was waiting, wagging its tail, nothing to be afraid of.

After maybe eight hours the apparition had grown to over a meter in height, doubled in brightness and the shape was clearly morphing into a humanoid figure. It then, after this extended period, disappeared. Rudy was horrified, he did not want it to leave him; after so many days, weeks and months he finally had a companion, which had then abruptly left him. He felt angry and let out a few words of wisdom not found in the flight manuals. The spectrum analyzer recordings did show a history of faint signals, but they were gone now.

"Rats... where... what was that," he exclaimed, talking for the first time in who knows how many days. "This is the best thing that has happened in a long, long time and now its gone. I can't even report it, they will take over the ship and return me to *Gaea*. Rats!"

Rudy was now, an hour later, still staring at the place where the translucent shape formed. Still upset about the departure, he tried to relax and eat another meal; he

161

noted the time that the form appeared and decided to wait until the next day in hopes of an encore. During the rest of his evening, Rudy checked systems and cleaned up, periodically looking in the direction of the navigation equipment, hoping to see it again. It would not appear that night.

The next day, Rudy reviewed the time of the first sighting and looked forward to another show, even though he knew it was irrational, this was the most excitement he had in a long time and he was determined to make the most of it, be it fiction or not.

At nineteen of the twenty four hours of waiting, the spectrum analyzer preset alarm went off. Rudy was just finishing his exercise period, which he had lost interest in recently, he moved over the the display panel and as he did, he looked towards the navigation equipment to find that the apparition had re-appeared. It was a bit brighter and more complete than the last appearance. There was a hint of sound as well. Rudy started the event recorders and moved slowly over to the left hand cockpit seat the view the apparition closer.

Relaxing and looking to its right, Rudy sat and watched, periodically checking instruments to try and discover what this phenomena was. He felt himself

162

unusually calm and comforted by the light, it felt warm and unassuming; a few more hours of watching allowed the light to form even more, the limbs to grow and a face with simple features to appear. It was magical to watch but after several hours, it again disappeared. Rudy was again very disappointed but felt somehow assured that the image would reappear as it had (now) a few times before. The next day, it was a bit more complete, a bit more bright, and in fact had made more noise. Humming maybe, maybe even a chord of low tones. This time is lasted a few minutes longer before it faded into nothingness.

Anticipating another visit, he prepared for the upcoming event by exercising a bit more enthusiastically and taking a long zero g shower.

Again, on about a nineteen hour cycle, she was back. Rudy felt this vision was female, but understood it might be wishful thinking. It *was* beautiful however, aquiline, serene, translucent and comforting. She was even looking at him every once in a while, this at the same time she looked about the cabin, sometime while pointing at a display or control panel. The sounds were even more pleasant this time, sometimes understandable as phases or intonations, like questions. The sound were so pleasant, Rudy did not leave her presence for want of more.

163

~*The Voyages of Gaea*~

At some point, Rudy finally understood the nineteen hour cycle, it was the rotational period of the planet. The spectrum analyzer recorded more signal strength, in fact it was an increase that, after a simple calculation, indicated that the signal was indeed emanating from the planet and every day's progress towards the planet gave a slight increase in signal intensity. It was starting to make sense, first the apparition was real and probably generated by a station on the planet and directed to the shuttle. Maybe it was a greeting or explorative beacon.

Over the next several days, she re-appeared, more defined and more articulate. She was beautiful, about the size of a small human female with many of the same morphological attributes. More and more, she gestured at the control panels and displays, pointing, then looking at Rudy quizzically. Rudy had the impression she was asking a question and started to explore a better way to communicate. He tried writing, drawing symbols, making sounds, making gestures, but to no avail. The apparition could not make sense of the attempts. At the same time, Rudy noticed the spectrum analyzer signals had more definition, like the shape of cell phone modulation. After some thought, he concluded that it was a modulation that could be replicated by the shuttle's communications

164

systems. He re-programmed the transmitters to create the same pattern as the ground station, and re-programmed the receivers to decode the pattern as well. This was almost identical to setting up a Wi-Fi on earth to create access to the Internet.

After the conversions were complete, Rudy reached over to the comm panel and attempted to engage the link. Instantly, the data transfer lights came to life, his companion looked directly at him and said:

"Hello, Rudy."

Rudy was stunned, the data link lights blinked very rapidly and various control panels went through self check routines. He started to become anxious about the activity.

"Its....OK, do not....worry, I am just trying to communicate with you more efficiently," she said. "It will take only a few....moments."

"All right," he said hesitatingly, "you may proceed, just don't do anything dangerous."

He realized that was probably a very undefined command, right after he said it. But a bit more patience would not hurt, especially if he needed to terminate the comm link if something went wrong. He reviewed the procedure, including switching off the comm link and pointing the antenna away from the planet.

After several more seconds, she responded. "We're okay now, we have an understanding about you, please do not be afraid, we mean no harm. We are explorers just like you and were curious why you were coming to see us.

"Can you explain how you can appear before me, so far away?"

"It is much like your radar technology, we form a beam in your direction and shape it with energy, your computers have no record of this technology, so we have downloaded the details for you. It is a much faster way to explore, to project your image and sense the surroundings of another world or place, like your ship."

"Can you control this ship?"

"Only with your permission, we must remain absolutely passive, so as not to cause you concern."

"Thats good."

She was now even more defined now, having taken advantage of better understanding of the comm systems and receiving equipment. Rudy felt very calm, much like basking in the afterglow with his girlfriend back home. Even though there was a complete lack of physical attraction, Rudy was mesmerized by her, fascinated by her movements, face, appendages.

Time was running out however, considering the

166

nineteen hour day.

"May I come back tomorrow, Rudy?"

"Of course, please."

Within a minute, the apparition was gone, Rudy in an instant was lonely for her. The shuttle was unusually quiet for a moment as his senses were reaching out like outstretched arms, trying to find something. After a bit of time, things returned to normal and the sound of the air movement equipment and cooling fans increased to their initially perceived levels. It was still quiet in some respects, but the knowledge that it would not remain so helped Rudy to concentrate on other aspects of space life.

There were still several weeks to go in the voyage and it soon became necessary to prepare for a landing. She visited for several hours every day to talk about her people and ask about his. The conversations covered religion, philosophy, science, personal relationships and everyday activity. Her planet was more advanced than Earth in many ways, but not so much as to not see the path from our level of understanding to theirs. Interestingly, they had chosen to live in the deserts and oceans, giving what animals they had left (after their industrial period) back to the land. They had reversed their birth rates to lower their swelled population and each newborn child was introduced

167

with a celebration and a plethora of uncles and aunts to raise them. They lived solely off of the energy of their sun, which included its light and influences on the wind and tides.

He found one other interesting piece of information about her people, they had no gender, or maybe more accurately, thousands of genders. There was a smooth continuum between more male and more female attributes, but no distinct dividing lines. There were many shared physical attributes, more male like people could nurse and had the equivalent of hormonal cycles. More female like people were stronger and more aggressive. The center two thirds of the population could give birth. In rare cases, even asexual reproduction had occurred. She of course was fascinated by the fact that Earth people had no such gender spectrum.

"Doesn't this cause problems?" She asked one time.

"Yes, of course, but there is some blending."

"Interesting."

"How do you pick a mate?" He asked.

"You pick one based on your interests."

"Do you have a mate?" he inquired.

"No....but I would like to be yours."

168

Rudy had initially been frozen by this revelation from her, but after a moment felt no concern about a decision.

"Sure, that would be wonderful."

"We will meet on the surface, after you land."

"How will I know you from the others?"

"There is only one me."

The shuttle, while in preparation for landing, received significant amounts of information about the new planet, much of which was then uploaded to the very distant *Gaea*. By now the mother ship was months away in flight time, but Rudy had made a transition of sorts, feeling so comfortable with her and with the every growing image of the planet in the windshield.

The day soon came when all was secured for a landing, he strapped in, fired the retro rockets to slow down the shuttle and soon met the atmosphere. The buffeting was tolerable and the new planet had a beacon to fly towards for a landing. From high in the air, the planet was beautiful and serene, with weather much like back on Earth. He flew he craft towards the landing area, slowing down as he did. After several minutes, he found a large pad, surrounded by small buildings. It had markings on it that appeared to show the direction of the wind. He flew the

169

shuttle in a long arc to intercept the main mark on the pad and slowly approached it, making a smooth touch down. The atmosphere was breathable, warm, with much more oxygen. He equalized the pressure in the shuttle, smelling the new air as it replaced the months old stale air from the trip. Electrical systems were shut down for the first time in months, which caused a momentary fogging of the windshield. After a few minutes of throwing switches, Rudy looked up through a clearing windshield to find the inhabitants looking at him from a distance, near some small buildings. They were much like her, only they could walk; large eyes, beautiful lines, lithe but complete. For a moment he panicked, concerned he would not be able to recognize her. Soon though, after some study, he realized they were all, in a way, different.

A small group approached the shuttle, whose systems were still winding down, and waited for the door to open. By this time, the landing checklist was complete and Rudy, although in a spacesuit, realized a helmet was not necessary and opened the door to meet the new people.

Once the door was fully open, he stepped out and raised his hand in greeting. Slowly the inhabitants responded with the same gesture. One of the Benthans moved forward and spoke.

170

"Welcome to our planet, Rudy. Your mate is waiting for you."

"Thank you, you speak my language."

"We learned it from our delegate, Zsa, who was projected onto your ship. Your gracious permission to allow us to see your computer files also helped us to understand your culture and level of technology. It also allowed us to learn your language."

"Your welcome, I am here to represent our world and learn about yours. The delegate, as you call her, was very helpful to me and I am anxious to get to meet her in person."

"Of course, please follow us. You may stay as long as you want on our world. We will provide you with the food and staples you need if you decide to return to your people."

"Thank you, that is much appreciated."

The group, including Rudy, walked toward one of the outlying buildings. Slow but at a very steady pace. The Benthans moved in synchrony, almost in harmony. The architecture of the surrounding buildings also had a feeling of harmony. Rudy again had that overwhelming feeling of comfort, just like he had in the presence of Zsa. They led him into a building with smooth rounded walls, past small rooms then into a larger room, maybe 20 meters on a side.

171

Near the center was a table and rounded chairs. These chairs were shaped to fit the Benthans, not too uncomfortable for a Terran, but different. He sat down, while in unison, the welcoming committee moved away in different directions to retrieve food and drink. They return in unison, place the food and drink around Rudy in unison and sat in unison. One spoke:

"Your mind moves slower than ours."

"I am just trying to absorb the new surroundings....and the unexpected pleasure of being able to talk to you in my native tongue."

"Actually, now that you are here, we can sense that the electrical impulses in what you refer to as your brain, move at a much lower frequency than our own. We can fix the defect for you if you would like."

"Oh, actually, thats ok," said Rudy.

For the first time, he felt a bit uneasy. Either the look on his face or the change in electrical activity in his brain caused the assembled group to recoil a bit.

"We sense anxiety, please understand we mean no harm."

"Ok."

"Please....eat....and drink."

Rudy, slowly at first, examined his food and drink.

172

The fluid in the glass appeared to be water, he sipped, it was water but better, like artesian water from the mountains of Earth. He drank a bit more, thinking about the last time, as a young boy, he drank the pure waters in the mountains of New Mexico, with his family. He smiled involuntarily.

"Beautiful," said one the of Benthans, who then closed her eyes (she looked more feminine).

"What?" Rudy asked.

"That was a beautiful image, it smelled wonderful....and the sounds of the forest!"

Rudy stopped for a moment, looked around the room and found that many of the "committee" had closed their eyes.

It took a while but soon Rudy understood that they were telepathic; so advanced mentally that they had the ability to sense the electrical impulses of nearby people, interpreting them as well.

"You can read my mind?"

"Well, more accurately, see your images. Sounds are one dimensional, images are four dimensional. There is more energy with the images and we sense them first. In the background are the other senses. Were you standing when you drank this water in the mountains?"

"I don't remember."

173

"He was," said another Benthan. "He had blue pants, a red shirt, white shoes...."

"Blue jeans and sneakers."

They looked at him quizzically. New words for them, not in the digital archives. Another closed eyed Benthan said:

"You woke up because you heard a noise...to your left. It rained later that day. Your....mother.....asked you to help with the dishes. You put them in the stream and used the sand in the stream to clean the plates and.....pot. You arose....to your left, the sun was 30 degrees above the horizon, you saw a bird fly....right to left. You took a breath, placed your right foot in front of you and...."

"You can see all of that?"

The Benthans again sensed anxiety, recoiled a bit.

"We will stop now. Your brain has significant detail about all of your experiences. The transport method to get your memories to your consciousness is not...optimal. We can fix that as well."

"Oh, sounds interesting, I'll have to think about that. I am concerned that such a dramatic change in me would change my life too much....and cause problems."

"As you wish."

"Where is....Zsa?"

174

"When you are replenished, we will take you to her."

Too excited to finish his food, Rudy took a few quick bites, which caused some of the Benthans to become very interested. He cleaned up with a napkin, took a last sip of the good water and feeling the need to be mobile, pushed back his chair and rose.

The Benthans did not expect the pace of the interaction with Rudy to quicken to such a degree. Their harmony was disturbed and they were motionless until their synchrony re-established itself.

At once, they all rose, the leader of the group moved to the "point" position and they, with Rudy moved out of the room and down a long hall. Several rooms were passed on the way, mostly with simple arrangements inside or bare. The color was a consistent off white, the walls glowed to provide light, the floor, always level. They moved from the hall to an arcing, outside walkway. Their sun was out and pleasant. Past the walkway, they re-entered the building to a more serious looking area. There were more pieces of furniture and the walls had significantly more detail, including image screens and control panels.

"This might be the science area," thought Rudy.

"You are right," a voice in Rudy's head said.

Now he was getting concerned, looked around the

175

small crowd to try to understand who had entered his mind and spoke to him. The privacy of his thoughts were gone, he realized.

"We will stop," another voice in his mind said.

"Thanks."

The moved through the science area and soon entered a large room with a significant amount of equipment, tended to by (for the first time) people in different clothing.

"She is here."

"Where?"

"Here," one of the Benthans moved over to a bench with several objects on it, carefully picked up an orb of glass, with what initially appeared to be sea weed in it. He turned to Rudy, moved closer and handed the orb to him.

Rudy carefully took the sphere, some 20 centimeters in diameter, looked at it , then the person who had given it to him.

"I don't understand."

"Zsa sacrificed her physical being to be programmed into this information sphere."

As the person described the process of the transformation, Rudy felt a warming, not in his hands, but in his mind.

176

"We eliminated the matter and programmed all that Zsa is into this memory orb. Only then could she travel along our sensor probes that met you so long ago in space. She is here (as he looked at the orb) and wants to spend the rest of her life with you."

Rudy was overtaken. Her image as a beautiful person, perfect in every way, was present in his mind. For a moment, she was at the mountain stream, helping him clean the dishes. She looked up and smiled.

"Can she read my mind?"

"She is as real as you allow her to be, and will be your companion forever. Many of our people considered this role for you. She was best suited and most interested in being with you."

"How does she....will she ever...."

"All of your questions will be answered, by her, over time."

Rudy needed to sit down, a chair appeared, Zsa spoke to him."

"Please sit, Rudy. I will take care of you, no harm will ever come to you. You are getting tired, you may give me back to them. We will arrange for you to rest."

Rudy was in fact exhausted, mostly mentally from the new experiences of interacting with the Benthans. The shock of meeting Zsa took its toll as well. They led him to a quiet room, with a window and a bed. He sat at the edge of the bed, and as he did the Benthans started to leave. Zsa was placed on a circular ring, in the center of the room.

"Rest, my love."

Eyes at half mast, Rudy laid down and within seconds was asleep. The farther the Benthans got from the room the less his mind was active, the effect was overwhelming. Soon he began to dream.

His dreams were of her and the bountiful life he would live from now until forever. Every image however misty and obscure, had her in the background, observing. A few times over the next several hours, he awoke with a clear memory of a dream, always with some metaphorical story, always with her in the scene.

Hours later, he awoke for good. Rising from his bed, he wandered over the the window to look out and reaching out to the back of his neck and felt a slight headache. Nothing special, just there.

"Here, I'll fix that," came a voice in his mind.

The slight headache was removed and replaced by a peaceful sensation.

Rudy turned left and looking down a bit, stared at the orb, still slightly luminescent. Blanking his mind

178

intentionally, he walked out of the room, turned right and walked down a hallway. Every meter away from his room gave a strange sense of relief, followed by the return of the headache. He continued as far as he felt comfortable, just until he had alerted the local Benthans of his presence. They moved to join him and gently escorted him back to his room.

"You strayed too far from Zsa, she is sad."

"Humans need to be alone every once in a while, or they become stressed. I just spent a significant amount of time alone in a space vessel and am having a hard time with all of the intrusions into my mind."

"We don't understand, everyone here feels comforted by the presence of the others. You should feel the same way."

"I don't, our species is not used to voices in our mind, it will take a while to get used to it."

"Please return to your room, Zsa is sad."

"Okay."

Rudy walked back to his room, looked at the orb near the center and noticed it was not as luminescent as when he had left. The mental sensations came back to him, but no voices or images. He sat down on the edge of the bed to consider what to do.

179

"Why did you leave me?"

"I didn't leave you, I went for a walk."

"I sense you are uncomfortable here, do you want to leave again?"

"Zsa, the voices make me uncomfortable. I am not going to be able to stay here long, can we see more of your world?"

"Of course."

Instantly, Rudy had images of the country, oceans, mountains and parks. Rudy recoiled.

"No, not like that....for real."

"But its so....inefficient."

"I understand, but its an intrusion for humans."

The images disappeared, to Rudy's relief. He thought for a moment, looking out the window, he paused.

"Zsa, we have to make a decision....."

"Okay."

"Do you have in your memory, the history of your people and details of your world?"

"I do, every detail, as I was transformed into memory data I also assimilated all of our cultural history."

"Good, we need to leave."

"As you wish."

"I have another question.....can you return to your

corporeal self?"

"The process I underwent required a machine that mapped each of my molecules, it used what you refer to as X-rays. The mapping was complete down to the detail of the position and type of each molecule. My mind is complete in every detail because of this. These data are stored in perfect detail within this sphere. It can be transferred to a compatible data bank for re-assimilation if you have the technology onboard *Gaea*. For now I can communicate with you through your mind when you are close, or through the computer system on your spacecraft."

"Excellent. I enjoy your people and your planet, but your ability to communicate directly to my mind is, for now, uncomfortable. We humans are too used to the privacy of our own thoughts. I think I can get used to communicating with you Zsa, but the presence of so many of your people talking to me or listening to me at once is overwhelming. If you have details of your culture and history, I have obtained what I came here for. And more if you come with me back to my home. We will always be able to communicate with your people and if you wish, you may return home someday. For now however, I think it is time to leave."

"I am committed to being with you forever and look forward to meeting your people. We may leave at your discretion."

"Zsa, I appreciate your sacrifice and I will take care of you."

Having brought very little, Rudy gathered his things and carefully picked up Zsa. Looking into the sphere, he saw movement and a luminescent glow. Smiling, he held it firmly and walked towards the door to the room. Turning right, he walked down the hallway towards the opening that led to the pad where the shuttle was parked. The inhabitants of Benthic 2 sensed his departure, moved aside as he walked and bid him farewell. Rudy walked out of the building in which he had barely spent a full day and into the sunshine. It was clear outside, with a light breeze. Rudy noticed the lack of familiar sounds from Earth, replaced only by mechanical humming and the wind. He protected the sphere he held from direct sunlight and approaching the shuttle, opened the hatch remotely and placed the sphere inside the doorway before he entered.

He walked up the air stairs, entered and turning left reached over and pressed a switch to retract the stairs and turn on the interior lights. Reaching down to his left, he picked up Zsa and moved toward the cockpit. Looking around he found a suitable safe place near the center where the sphere would be held carefully but firmly enough

182

to safely endure any turbulence during the launch and climb out.

Thanking himself for the intensive training, he sat down, switching on the battery power before he got comfortable. Looking up at the overhead panel he used his right hand to start the auxiliary power unit. He left hand reached for the control arm, much like a collective in a helicopter and pushed the starter enable button for the engines. Rudy then found the checklist and quickly brought the engines on line, switched in the electrical and hydraulic power, then switched on the avionics master.

The ship quickly came to power, display screens flicked to life, reset and system confirmation lights blinked. He brought the power up to enable a hover while finishing the before takeoff checklist. Turning the craft clockwise and setting the flight director to 10,000 feet, he advanced the thrust levers to increase speed.

The environmental systems came on line, pressurizing the spacecraft and controlling the temperature. All systems came activated flawlessly as the climb out proceeded to an orbital entry phase. The whole process from hatch closure to flight took about four minutes, much faster than required but enough to allow Rudy to get comfortable in his quest to leave the planet.

183

It wasn't that bad of a place, the people were very gracious and welcoming. It was just, their advanced brainpower allowed them to be in his mind, something he had not experienced before. Maybe someday the Terrans would be better prepared for this kind of interaction, but for now it was still very invasive.

"We're outta here!"

No response.

"Zsa, are you still with me?"

No response.

Rudy engaged the autopilot for the rest of the climb out and orbital insertion. He turned his attention to the sphere.

"Zsa? Are you still with me?"

No response.

Rudy started to get concerned, he felt bad that in his haste to depart the planet he might have forgotten something important about moving Zsa. He looked closely at the sphere, the internal contents were still luminescent and moving. He thought about the environment, the temperature, air pressure, humidity; but all was in order, just like the planet's. Then is dawned on him, Zsa had only communicated through their radar beams while he was in transit to the planet. Those beams were gone now, but how

184

could he replicate the same equipment. On her planet, there must have been other fields of energy that enabled her to communicate with him. Now he had to figure out the problem of getting her to communicate with him again.

But first there was the issue of established a flight plan back home, home to *Gaea*. The navigation systems needed to orient themselves again and give him the proper vectors for a homeward trajectory. This took some time, but after Rudy settled into spaceflight mode and finished his check lists, the nav systems were ready and he engaged the flight management system to take him back to his home. The shuttle had increased its speed to the proper cruise velocity and the flight director main display indicated that the auto pilot had locked onto the proper course.

Settling back, he looked to his right and finding the sphere and thought about Zsa. He missed her already, even though it had been only a few hours. The first thing to do was review the sensor logs and try to enable the radar beams that had produced her image.

He had much of the proper equipment to do this but realized he had to design and build several interface circuits to get it to work properly.

"I've got nothing but time," he thought. "Like five and a half months."

Rudy paused to think about the extra long return voyage. Luckily the Benthans had replaced much of his food stocks during his short stay. In fact they had left food, electronic records of their world and a few unmarked containers neatly stowed away in the farthest reaches of the shuttle.

"I wonder what those boxes contain?"

Rudy spent the next several hours uncovering and examining the "gifts." He decided however, after looking carefully at the unmarked containers, that they would not help his quest to see Zsa again and returned to his interface design work. This took several days to complete, but once he was done, he was eager to test the system to see if it would work.

He brought the sphere over to the new electronics boards, placed it carefully in a padded ring of electrodes and connected the board to the computer system onboard the shuttle.

"Well, here goes."

He turned on the the power supplies that fed the interface boards and waited to see if any signals were coming out of the sphere. Within seconds, there were indications of significant activity, as if the sphere had detected the interface circuitry, not the other way around.

186

"Thats interesting," he thought. "I wonder how...."

All of a sudden, there was a flash of images on the shuttle computer's displays. Jumbled and quickly changing, like the rolling images of a broken television set from the past.

"Wow, what's this?"

Sound starting coming over the shuttle intercom system as well, jumbled and noisy, but with snippets of voices. The interface circuitry was working at maximum speed, drawing large amounts of current from the power supplies.

The noise on the speakers stopped, the images on the displays slowed to something more visually manageable.

"Rudy?"

"Zsa?"

"Rudy? I can't hear you, are you there?"

"Zsa? Stand by."

Rudy reached over the pilot's seat and grabbing his headphones, plugged them into the closest socket. He adjusted the microphone to be close to his mouth.

"Zsa? Are you there? Zsa?"

A moment of silence, a flickering of current.

"Rudy, I can hear you, your in port six of the

computer audio terminal panel."

For some reason, this made Rudy smile.

"No actually, I am sitting down in front of the panel, I have plugged a microphone in the panel, that's why you think I am inside."

"Oh, I understand. But I can not see you. I am connected to your main computer and can tell that we are on our way back to your home. We left quickly, didn't we?"

"Yes, we did Zsa. After we made our decision, we were on our way back to *Gaea* within twenty minutes. Zsa, search the computer files for a folder labeled 'Internal Video', open it and start a program labeled 'cockpit cameras', tell me when you have done this."

"Ok, stand by....ok the program has been located and initiated...stand by.....I have multiple views of you working near my sphere."

"Perfect, that will help you see what I am doing. By the way, did you have image projectors back on your world?"

"We do, that is how you could hear me and see the others."

"See the others? Those people I interacted with weren't real?"

"Most of them were projections, a few were real."

188

"Wow, they had amazing details, why do some of them prefer to be projected?"

"They can move faster and learn more quickly, we discovered that assimilating into a computer systems and leaving our biological parts behind allows us to live forever and truly fulfill our lives."

"And...some prefer not to be projected, or assimilated into a computer?"

"They...we... are not interested in an unreal existence, even if it means being what you refer to as mortal. In the world of computers and energy, feelings are not real, only sensations. Thoughts are not your own, but shared with everyone, many of the less capable of our society chose to become digitized, it was a lot easier. In my group, we felt that the extra burden of biological life and having our own thoughts was far more attractive. We are in the minority however...and loosing people all of the time. The end result of this digital life is to be contained in a memory sphere."

"But why did you make the transformation?"

"Your shuttle was the first outside contact we have had in many, many years. The ruling council thought it would be best if a real person with real feelings was digitized and projected to you, both for us to determine your

189

intent and for us to get to know you."

"What if my intent was hostile?"

"We would have vaporized you."

This realization sobered up Rudy. He did not need to question her sincerity, he had witnessed a very advanced society with the ability of projecting images over millions of miles. No doubt they could have defended themselves.

Rudy finally spoke:

"I believe that you could....but I am still interested in why you made a decision to sacrifice your corporeal self."

"A group of finalists was selected, we were asked to study what we had learned from our probes. I found that after looking at all of the information, that I had a particular attraction to Terrans and you in particular."

"I'm honored."

"Thank you."

"Zsa, I need to get back to work and figure out a way to project you like your radar probes did when I was coming to your world."

"I can help. I am connected to your computer system and can now instruct you on how to make the projection system."

Rudy had Zsa show the details of the projector on the shuttle display screens. He gathered the required

190

equipment and started to assemble the unit. He worked in silence, methodically wiring up the circuit cards and projection modules. It took several days of work but ultimately the unit was completed and he started the tests. At first, the projector could display a two dimensional image in black in white. After adjustments and software modifications, the image quality progressed and became more and more three dimensional. The resolution also improved.

"I look good." Zsa said one day, breaking a long silence.

"You do, I have some more adjustments to make but we are getting there."

"Actually, I can do it from inside the computer. Stand by," she said.

Rudy relaxed a bit from his labors and watched as her image became clearer. Then in what appeared to be a magical transformation, the image looked as real as real gets. In fact, scarey real. He thought the rest of his senses came alive as well. He could smell, see and hear her. Her image seemed to actually bounce off of the control panels as she floated gracefully about the cockpit.

"Thats amazing."

"Am I real now?"

"Undoubtably."

She found her way to the co-pilots seat and nuzzled in. Rudy followed suit into the captain's seat. They had a lot of time to talk.

Over the next many weeks, they talked, communicated with *Gaea*, reviewed their respective worlds' histories and cultures...and again became as close as they had on the inbound journey. She stayed awake all of the time, watching the systems and keeping them safe.

Again, what seemed like a few weeks actually was several months. *Gaea's* beacon signals gained in strength on a daily basis. Before long, they had turned the shuttle around to begin the retro rocket firings and approach process. At this point they had but a few days before meeting up with the giant spaceship. Zsa had assimilated a significant amount of information regarding Terrans. She became concerned about how they would react to her. Rudy tried to re-assure her but she knew their curiosity would drive them to examine her in detail.

"I'm concerned, more so than I have ever been, Rudy. I keep track of the intranet traffic on *Gaea* and they are making a significant amount of plans for me after we arrive."

"They're just interested to meet you. You're very

192

advanced relative to them and they want to get to know you, that's all."

"I'm not so sure. I read your report to them last week, they formed a committee to discuss the details and have informed the psychotherapists that they will be busy after we arrive."

"I didn't know that, but I still think that is normal, considering I have spent the last six and half months essentially in a shuttle. They probably are concerned about the long term effects of solo space flight."

"I think they are very concerned."

"Well Zsa, I still think it will be ok. I am actually looking forward to seeing them again, and introducing you to my friends."

"Speaking of friends, I've noticed that you do not communicate with them very often, they send messages to you but do not receive a response until much later. Are you not close to them?"

"Oh, I am. It just that being with you has satisfied all of my social needs. We have talked about so much. Your personality is so amazing that sometimes I care little about anything else but being with you."

"Well, things are about to change," she said carefully.

193

~*The Voyages of Gaea*~

As if on cue, the shuttle's autopilot was taken over by the remote piloting systems onboard *Gaea*. The craft eased about and changed directions slightly. Rudy was pleased that he had navigated so many millions of miles and upon return had only been off by less than a mile. He smiled at this and was comforted by the fact that the remote piloting would guide his flight through the final stages to landing. Traffic control was in constant contact with the shuttle now, both verbally and electronically, refining system settings and environmental controls.

The great spacecraft was in view by now, starting out as a small bright object straight ahead, growing in size every hour until it filled the windows. The shuttle was slowed to an approach speed, lined up with the final vectors to enter the shuttle bay and just before touchdown, the landing gear was deployed. The shuttle entered the landing bay, Rudy saw his first Terrans in months through the protective glass panels, he waved. Minutes later, the bay doors were closing and the shuttle settled softly onto the landing pad. Voices in the cockpit told Rudy to be patient as the air was introduced into the landing bay, this took several minutes. Finally, the ok was given and a flock of support personnel moved quickly out to the shuttle. Rudy, unbuckled now, rose and walked to the cabin door. The first switch he threw equalized the pressure in the shuttle to the outside ambient pressure. The second switch initiated the air stair system.

The door opened with a slight hiss, Rudy looked down and smiled at a small crowd of technicians and scientists.

"Welcome home. How do you feel?"

"I feel great, what a wonderful voyage. Wait 'til you see what I brought with me."

He descended the air stair and feeling the gravity again, moved slowly toward the awaiting crowd. They embraced him and assisted him into an electric cart. Technicians immediately started to attach umbilical cords to the shuttle and entered to view the interior. They did this with great care.

"Be careful, there is someone in there, keep the systems on and you will see her."

"We know, we will be careful, don't worry. First we need to get you to sick bay for a thorough examination. After that will be a full mission debrief."

"Can Zsa come with me?"

"Not at this time. We need to understand her.....projection system first. Then maybe later."

"Ok," Rudy said, feeling a bit lonely even though he

was surrounded by ship's personnel."

The electric cart, with technicians in tow, moved down the hallways of *Gaea*, people moved aside and smiled at Rudy. He waved and said hello to some, he was content to be home. Soon he was in sick bay, his flight physician greeted him and several of the psychology department personnel were there also.

"We will help you onto the examination table, we need to do a complete check up."

"Thank you, I feel great. Its nice to be home."

"You had quite a journey, many months in fact. We have a complete set of data on your well being. You exercised well, ate well. All in all, we were very pleased with your discipline."

"Thank you, I had help. Would you like to meet her?"

"No, not quite yet. We need to take care of you first."

"Ok. But, she is being taken care of, right?"

"Oh, yes, she is in fine shape. Very safe. Ok, look straight ahead while I examine your retinas........"

He was in sick bay for two hours, the first two thirds was a medical exam and the last third was some basic conversations with the psych staff. Easy questions really, they acknowledged that his voyage was made much easier because of his companion. It was very difficult until her appearance on the initial part his voyage, after which time his blood pressure and general overall health improved.

After the sickbay, Rudy, with assistance, walked slowly to a nearby conference room for the debriefing session. He sat down to food and drink, the room had several people in it already but soon filled. People sat down, looking at Rudy.   The last person in was the spacecraft commander, who walked over and shook Rudy's hand.

"Welcome home."

"Thank you, its great to be back. I hope you feel that the mission was a great success, I certainly do. I brought back a great deal of information about the inhabitants of Benthic 2. They are very advanced, they have learned to combine their biological selves with advanced technological equipment. Many of them are just projections."

A mission commander, responsible for much of Rudy's voyage took over.

"Rudy, we have done a preliminary review of your ship's logs and have a few questions. But first, we want to welcome you back and thank you for a very successful

197

research mission. The data you acquired will be immensely helpful to us. We have data on the climate, geography and seas of this planet. The automatic sensors have brought back many terabytes of information; it will take months to fully appreciate what you did. But first a few fundamental questions."

"Ok, go ahead."

"Rudy, the flight log indicated that you flew to this planet, orbited it once and flew back to *Gaea*, can you explain why?"

"Oh, no, that's not what happened, we landed........"

"We?"

"Yes, Zsa and I, we landed....I disembarked and met the inhabitants. They had prepared for our arrival, spoke english in fact. We spoke for a while and they brought me into one of their buildings. After a few hours there, I felt tired and they allowed me to sleep in one of their rooms. Zsa was there. As I said, they are an advanced society and have learned to map the chemical and electrical activity in their brains, so, many times you do not see them speak, but you hear their voices. They easily read my mind. In fact, it became uncomfortable to me as they knew what I was thinking at all times. It was also not easy for me to hear them talk in my mind. We chose to leave and I found out

198

that the range of their "mind reading" was limited. The further away we got, as we walked towards the shuttle for a return flight, the quieter it became. I was just too much for me, so I had to leave quickly."

"Ok, so you stayed for about a day?"

"That is correct, twenty two hours in fact."

"Hmmm. Ok. And, uh, as far as Zsa is concerned, can you tell me about her?"

"Why yes, she is my companion. They broadcast her on board the shuttle when I got reasonably close. They used their equivalent of our radar beams to project an image, amorphous initially, into the cockpit. They did this to learn about my intentions, and whether I was a threat or not."

"She was allowed access to the shuttle's computer?"

"Yes, I made that decision once I determined *they* were not a threat."

"Ok....your ship's logs do not indicated such a connection, can you explain that?"

"No....not yet."

"And you say that you brought her back?"

"Yes, she is in the shuttle, in a glass sphere. You will find an interface board connected to the ship's computers. It took me a while to design and perfect, but the image is now very clear. Have you found her?"

"Not yet, early reports from the ramp technicians indicate the shuttle was a bit of a mess, its hard to understand some of your wiring and auxiliary circuitry. But we'll get there. So, no, we have not found her. You say that you had an interface board connected to the computers. How did you project the image?"

"I used components from the main radar system and some special circuits to make it work."

"Ok, we will look for those....and her." He looked up at Rudy as he said this.

The de-briefing went on for another hour and was cut short because Rudy was exhausted. The electric cart was used to take Rudy back to his quarters. He was able to walk from the hallway into his living area. Saying "goodbye" to the medical staff that had accompanied him, he went inside and closed the door. The fatigue was overwhelming. Instead of calling his friends, he walked into the kitchen, opened a beer and proceeded to go to the bedroom for rest. The gravity of the ship was more that he had experienced in some time, Benthic 2 was somewhat smaller that Earth and as a consequence had about 80% the gravity. The shuttle made gravity artificially but nothing close to that which was burdening him now. He took a sip of beer, and sitting on the side of the bed, placed the drink on the night table. Within seconds, he had rolled to his side, onto the pillow and fell asleep.

He dreamt of Zsa, wonderful images at first, conversations about anything he wanted to talk about, her comforting style and attention to his words. The dreams changed to anxious thoughts of having lost her and finally a nightmare of her demise at the hands of *Gaea's* engineers and technicians.

He woke up with a start. The room was dark, the loud sounds of the shuttle had been replaced by the quite murmurs of the much larger ship. He sat up on the edge of the bed, trying to clear his mind and understand the questions of the de-briefing committee. Why had they not found her? Why were they acting in such a reserved fashion, especially the psychotherapists? Did they think she was not real? Rudy was now awake and a bit agitated.

"Zsa?"

Silence. "Zsa, are you there?"

"I am here my love."

SUSCEPTANCE

"There was no fuss or fanfare; switches were set; recorders started and the data began to flow"

– John Kraus, after the completion of the 360' radio telescope

~*The Voyages of Gaea*~

The astronomy wing of *Gaea* was getting annoyed. Matt, a young promising observer, was making maps of a particular star system with *Gaea's* best equipment and talking about unusual findings. The other astronomers were very busy and hoped Matt would figure out if it was real or if it was equipment problems quickly. They needed to know quickly.

But Matt was insistent, claiming he wasn't getting any help on a legitimate problem. He went to his supervisor.

"Eliot, I have been over the measurements several times. I also checked the smaller telescopes that were looking at the same field, they saw the same thing."

"Did you do the calibrations correctly?"

"Once before and once after. I even performed a cal this morning. All seems normal, but the holes are still there."

"Hmmm, ok, well I have to finish a paper and a proposal tonight so I can't help you until tomorrow sometime. I would really like to see my family for a bit."

"Ok, thanks Eliot, I understand you are really busy, but I have checked the literature and talked to several other people, they all told me to contact you."

"No problem, happy to help if I can. Talk to you

tomorrow."

"Okay."

He was still frustrated though, the data were so unusual that it demanded immediate attention. Matt had to relax, the data would not change in the next 24 hours. Slowly he went back to his cabin. Once there he ate a nice meal, invited his girlfriend over to talk about some of the details of his research and tried to relax. At some point he looked at her and considered what depths his fecundity could reside, but left the decision to the future. She smiled at him, which did nothing to dissipate the allure. His mind was however pulled back to reality at some point.

"I'm sitting on something huge, and people are busy."

"What is it?"

He sat up and looked at Annlee straight in her eyes, almost through her.

"I have been looking at this particular star field for the last many weeks. I've looked at many, many star fields over the years, but this one is completely unique. It has holes in."

"Holes in it, I don't understand."

"Yeah, holes, in other words, I use the telescopes to measure the temperatures of the stars and star systems and the measurements range from many hundreds to several hundreds of thousands of degrees. Astronomers have been doing this for years, we can examine stellar birth grounds and supernovas or the cool outlying planets of a large solar system using this technique. But no one has every seen anything like what I have found. The holes are areas of very low temperature so they appear like black spots on my displays and they can be found on several of the planets and even some of the moons. In fact there is one or two that appear like they are just floating in space."

"Are you sure the equipment is working properly?"

"Of course, I've used several telescopes, calibrated them all. This phenomenon is just in this particular solar system. And... the peculiar thing about this is that the holes change."

"Like...move?"

"No, the holes appear and disappear in the same place, kind of randomly."

He sat back to consider his words, she sat back as well, understanding to some degree that what he was seeing was important but not the complete import of it.

"Have you told anyone about this?"

"Sort of, I started talking to Eliot, but he is so busy that I could not go into any detail."

205

"I'm sorry, but I'm sure it can wait."

"I don't know, I really could use some answers now, its just that....."

"Lets go the the beach."

"Oh, I don't....."

"Come on, it will be relaxing."

The "beach" was actually an auditorium size room, a few levels down and near a series of relaxation areas, meant to be a reminder of the beauties of home. The room was very large, domed, thirty meters high. The walls and ceiling were actually large image displays, very high resolution. There was a long pile of sand and warm water with a hidden wave machine. A few beach chairs were placed near the center. With the displays on, it was very realistic. When the wind came up, white sheets of fine sand levitated and moved out to sea, The birds were there, the sounds and the smell of salt air. After a few minutes, your mind was completely convinced of the experience.

Matt and Annlee reserved the beach for three hours, took some beach towels and walked down the corridors to the room. Once there they entered, closed and locked the doors and started to relax. They talked to the first hour, about most anything except the astronomical findings. The second hour was mostly quite, listening to the surf and smelling the fresh air, much like that after a rainstorm. The sea birds aligned themselves into the off shore winds, ruffling their feathers every once in a while. A distant thunderstorm sparked brilliant lightning displays followed by the hollowed sounds of lightning. He entered the water, feeling the relief of gravity upon his frame. The waves bobbed him up and down, relaxing his spine and lessening the load on his mind. He stayed for a long while until dusk begat night, then he came out of the water and dried off. The lightning displays were still fascinating, even after another thirty minutes. Matt and Annlee watched in silence. Then Matt, after another few minutes, sensed something odd. He watched the display and then the after images, where the light overwhelmed the retinal sensors and created a sensory deprivation for a moment after a strike. The sensation was like a dark after image, where the bright light once was. It reminded him of the dark spots in his astronomical readings.

"I'm done, I can't get away from this. I have to go back to work."

"Are you sure?"

"Yeah, I'm sorry. I just can't get this out of my mind. It's something really important."

A disappointed reply: "Ok, lets go."

207

They picked up their stuff, Annlee unhappy that Matt was unable to get away from work. Walking back, Matt was distant, they reached her quarters, he said goodbye and then after dropping off his beach wear in his cabin, walked back to the lab to continue his observations.

Once there, he reviewed his findings, consistent in every way, this particular solar system had holes that came and went. He measured the infrared properties again, the holes were colder than the surrounding areas and actually relatively small. The specific positions the holes were found and remained in the same areas of the sky.

He mulled over the data for a few hours, finally getting tired and returning to his quarters early in the morning. He slept soundly.

He awoke late in the morning, head still buzzing about his findings. His quarters bore the dishevelment of the previous night. Papers on the table, computer screens still showing the star fields, lights on in the kitchen. The front door was probably still open.

Dressed and somewhat awake, he walked back to his lab to maybe get a minute with one of the other astronomers. The lab was a mess too, technicians within looked about and wondered what had happened.

"Sorry about the mess."

208

"We were wondering what had happened."

Cleaning up the bits of paper, calculators and randomly placed computer displays, he offered an explanation. "I have been spending a lot of time of a data set from the large optical array. Just.....a lot of time."

"Something we can help with?"

"No, not.....well maybe, is there a chance you can do an independent calibration of the array? In visible through infra red?"

"Probably over lunch, if that works. We have a lot on our plate this morning."

"Thank you, that would be fantastic."

He finished his cleaning, remained polite to the technicians, who were going to go out of their way to do him a favor. Matt then waited for Eliot.

The day moved slowly, at about 1:30, one of the technicians sent a message from the large array, with the calibration numbers, flats and darks. Matt entered the numbers into the original data set for comparison against his original images. The holes were still there. He felt a bit better now with some independent confirmation, but was still anxious about understanding the meaning.

Near the late afternoon, when his energy was starting to wane, Eliot stopped by.

"I have a minute now, whatcha got?"

"Holes."

"Holes? What, in the space-time fabric? What kind of holes?"

"Holes. The absence of light, the absence of temperature, with the absence of a good explanation."

"Interesting, ok lets have a look. Go ahead and answer the questions you know I am going to ask." Eliot said, getting comfortable in front of a monitor screen.

"Ok, I calibrated several times, darks (no light into the telescope) and flats (uniform light into the telescope). I did it, and the technicians in my lab did it. The holes appear in a particular star field, same positions, on and off, nothing else like it in similar star fields, also used for calibration. The equipment checks out."

"Ok......you say the holes come and go.....do they do this in a periodic manner?"

"It seems random to me, but I can check over the long term."

"Perfect, take several 'holes' as you call them and run a Fourier analysis to see if they are periodic in any manner, lets do that now while I am here."

"Done," Matt said, happy that there were some more ways of thinking about the problem, happy that Eliot was helping him.

"Meanwhile, I am looking at the spectral data and noticing that the areas surrounding the holes are for the most part habitable, did you notice that?"

"Yes, I did, but I didn't think that was........."

"All except for the outliers, the ones not associated with a planet or moon, they appear to be surrounded by space, like a satellite. Did you check the proper motions?"

"Most of them, first I......."

"Lets do that again and make a comparison of motions vs. surrounding temperatures. I'll be back in an hour."

Eliot rose from the desk and quickly departed the lab, leaving Matt wondering what was going on. Within a few seconds, he was on task, filling in gaps in knowledge about the holes and trying to get the job done before Eliot returned.

Within fifty minutes, Eliot was back.

"Well, my family is upset, you might have to go my quarters and apologize to them."

"Be happy to, what happened?"

"I promised I would be home for dinner, got there and immediately went to work looking for something similar to this problem that I read about years ago. Holes, so to

211

speak. We need to take an ultra high resolution image of one of them. Can you predict their appearance yet?"

"Actually, yes, after I did the time study, there are several that show up like clockwork, how did you know?"

"Its in the literature, like so many other answers to interesting problems. How about the surrounding temperature profiles, find anything interesting?"

"Yes as well, the cooler ones move the fastest, in space. What's going on?"

"I will tell you after you get the hi-res image. Lets order it now, on a director's priority."

"Absolutely."

Matt went to the com panel and alerted the telescope operators that there was a director's priority image request, and gave them the coordinates. They complied instantly, stopping a survey by another observer, who wasn't particularly happy about it.

The image process took about an hour, from calibration to image to post calibration. The file was send directly to the lab Matt and Eliot were in.

They were finishing up a second cup of coffee when the file arrived.

"Do a point spread analysis on it," Eliot said.

"Ok, here goes.........huh....looks circular, uniform in

fact."

"Yep. I'm not surprised."

"Not surprised, why?"

"Because its a telescope."

"What? How could that be...how do you know?"

"This has happened before, in fact maybe even a few times before, but the data lacked the capabilities of our equipment we have here. Our proximity to the star system as well as our superior equipment gives us an incredible advantage. So think about it, here's what we have......a circular hole, with a lower temperature. Several holes in fact, some surrounded by Earth like temperatures, some floating in space, surrounded by space like temperatures...satellites. The lower temperatures inside the holes are a reflection of the cooled optics and imaging systems necessary to make good measurement....pictures if you will.

"Wow, thats right, thats amazing, they're telescopes, it all makes sense. But why are they......"

"They have detected us, the slow periodicities of the warmer surrounded holes are planets, their telescopes are tracking us on a 'nightly' basis. The cooler surroundings, in other words the satellites, are tracking us as well, but they go 'off target' to get their calibrations from other stars, stars

213

that are in fact behind us."

"Their tracking us, but why?"

"Well, because we are a 'discovery' to them, probably an incredible discovery. Think of what *Gaea* emits, light, thermal energy, electromagnetic energy."

Eliot laughed for a moment. "Think of the amount of papers being published on *us*."

Matt sat back in his chair, relieved that there was an answer but concerned about the implications. "What do you think they are going to do?"

"Hard to say, but I think its important that we do something."

"Like what?"

"Like communicate."

Matt smiled an evil smile. "Lets send them 'Star Trek' episodes from decades ago."

"Oh great, they'll think were Klingons with ray guns, nice idea," Eliot said with a smirk. "No, I was thinking about basic communications, starting a dialogue, calming their fears."

"Well if we must....how about images of nuclear bomb blasts from, like Bikini Island and Trinity and.....?"

"Your delirious, obviously you have not slept in several days. I tell you what, you go home to your girlfriend,

I will go home to my family. Before I go I will write up a short description of your discovery and sent it to the station managers. Nothing else can happen until tomorrow. Get some sleep, and meet me here at 0900."

"Ok, maybe your right. Goodnight"

"Goodnight, and by the way, good work."

"Thanks."

Matt, got up, looked at the cup of coffee, thought better of it and walked out of the lab. He felt stunned, amazed by the discovery, exhausted from the effort. He looked at people he passed in the corridors of the ship wondering what they would think once the story got out. He was proud...to a degree....proud of the results of his great effort. He was also sobered by the mystery of what the other civilization he discovered might think about this large ship, cruising through the cosmos, with all of the concomitant energy signatures.

He couldn't wait to tell Annlee, and walked directly to her quarters. Once there, he knocked on the door. It opened.

"I made an amazing discovery."

"I know."

"What? Nobody knows...yet."

"The technicians know or at least blogged that

215

something big was afoot."

"But they don't know the details...right?"

"No, just that something important was about to happen."

"Good, 'cause this is big, its huge...but I am not going to tell you until tomorrow."

"What? You can't do that, thats not fair...."

"Thats what you get for scaring me about the technicians."

"Okay, okay, come on lets have it, I won't tell anyone, won't even get on the computer."

"I don't know...its very important....I might get a raise."

"Please?"

"Promise you won't get on the computer or tell anyone until the details are released?"

"Promise."

"Ok.....here it is....another civilization is watching us."

Annlee walked over to the window and pulled down the shades.

"Watching us how?"

Smiling Matt said, "no its not like that that, they detected our presence and are wondering what we are, that's all."

"Are they dangerous?"

"Probably not, they're probably just very curious."

"How long have they been watching us?"

"Not long, they began their consistent observations just after I started taking images of their solar system. I was concerned about the 'holes' I was observing in the giant array data. It turns out that I was looking down the barrel of several of their telescopes. Eliot figured it out."

"Wow."

"I know, its pretty amazing. Eliot is writing up a preliminary report now, tomorrow the station managers will consider what to do. For now, its between us."

"Wow, thats amazing, so that's what was making you so anxious."

"Yeah, I couldn't let it rest. I went in to the lab last night and again this morning to make sure the readings were real. And they were real."

"What are we going to do about them?"

"Eliot wants to communicate with our new friends, I told him to send pictures of hydrogen bomb tests where we vaporized whole islands." He smiled at her.

"Well that's just dumb, that would scare them half......"

"Just kidding, I am so tired from this work that I was getting giddy. I need some sleep, but I had to tell you before anything else."

"Well, OK, I think. Now I get to stay up all night wondering what they're doing."

"Don't worry, I'm sure they mean no harm. I need to get some sleep. See you tomorrow?"

"Sure, goodnight, sleep well."

"Goodnight." He gave her his best smile, one of accomplishment and affection.

After a long well deserved peaceful sleep, he arose and discovered his e-mail alert was on. Reviving his laptop, he discovered the early rising managers had taken a keen interest in the news about the 'holes.'

"Meetings starting at nine," he observed.

He quickly got ready, made some tea, grabbed his backpack with his notes and computer and walked down to the first of several meetings. The halls were clean from last night's mopping and polishing. There was a faint smell of industrial floor cleaner in the air. The lights seemed brighter this morning, but he thought is was probably the result of so many days working on the 'hole' problem. He turned right at one of the many intersections and walked down another long passageway, until he came to a large conference room

218

usually reserved for upper management. This particular room was the property of the highest management level and usually unattainable by mere scientists.

"Classy," he thought walking into the room, which was partially filled with a mixture of people he knew and many he did not. The room had more wood work than normal, with the best projection equipment and much nicer chairs. He sat down in one, got nice and comfortable...

"Please, Matt, sit there," said someone pointing at an end chair, in view of all others.

He rose and changed positions, in a way not liking the prospects of being the center of attention.

The room filled up quickly including the addition of a few of those people who bring their own aura with them. Entering, they attract the attention of those who know them and those who do not.

Looking around the room he thought, "There's someone important,"

Soon the buzzing was over and a previously selected chairperson began to speak.

"Good morning. We have had an extraordinary discovery in the last several days by the astronomy team, led by Matt (he pointed) who is here to answer questions for us regarding the details. In addition, several other

219

supporting researchers are present today. But before we begin, I need to discuss the importance of this discovery not just in terms of this particular accomplishment but also in terms of the resulting applications of what we now call the "Matt algorithm." Unbeknownst to our intrepid discoverer (he pointed again), an application of his techniques and equations to previous observations have tripled the amount of intelligent life in the local star systems that we were aware of. Last night, after confirmation of his findings, another shift of researchers found significant evidence of similar "hole" phenomena across twenty two local star fields, which have at this point been assumed to be barren of life."

The commander of *Gaea*, who had slipped in a bit late and un-noticed, waited for a break in the conversation, and spoke:

"This is significant, our methods of finding life in the universe have been significantly improved with this discovery, nicely done Matt."

The room clapped, embarrassing Matt, who up to this point was comfortable with the anonymity. He nodded in thanks.

"Please continue," the commander said.

The chairperson picked up from where he had left

off, "What is interesting of course is that for the most part of our journey we have been observed, but not communicated with, unless its in a way we cannot readily discern. We need to think about this carefully. On the one hand, we might have been considered some simple astrophysical phenomenon, like a comet or asteroid. On the other, we need to consider how a civilization, with advanced astronomical equipment, would think of a resolvable image of a large starship, cruising across their heavens. Are these newly discovered civilizations aware of each other? For instance, Matt, can this techniques of yours work on ground based telescopes?"

"Well, I think so, first you need to consider......"

"Then we have just re-written history. Its important that the department heads convene study committees immediately to consider the impact of this discovery. We need to meet periodically to discuss our findings and obviously get teams on the old data. Lets get together weekly for at least the near term. Ok, let get started."

With that, the assembled members rose and vacated the room. Matt was one of the very last to get up, not understanding exactly what had just transpired. Standing, he looked around as everyone seemed to have an important task....except him. The room had quickly cleared and Matt walked out and not having an exact place to go. He decided to go back to his lab, hopefully to find Eliot to discuss what had just happened.

The halls seemed abuzz about the news, many people had been re-assigned to new tasks related to the discovery. A few people acknowledged Matt, as he slowly walked back to his lab.

He felt weird and in a way cold. Hours ago, he was proud of his work and now the impact of his findings caused a paradigm shift in his co-workers and many of the crew. He imagined that some people would be mad at having their routines changed or their fields of interest set aside for this seemingly more important work. But in reality, people were excited enough with the discovery to gladly move in a new direction. Matt was merely observing a paradigm shift.

With this new knowledge, he felt more comfortable and changed his gait to a saunter. He took in the looks and murmurs as he passed and decided he might even go home early today.

Epilogue

Years later, once Gaea had returned to Earth, Matt was considered a legend for his discovery. He returned to his home, settled in, found his old friends and relaxed. Of course, every once in a while he would pause to think about his future. This in terms of whether or not he would go further. The bane of so many researchers is looking back in time, even while they are still young, and wondering about the peak of their performance and whether or not those days are forever gone. The seasoned intellects always choose to keep the pace up, just in case they still have one left in them.

One evening, Matt went outside in his back yard, popped open a beer and once his eyes adjusted to the darkness, observed a satellite flying smoothly across the celestial sphere. Smiling he wondered if it was another Gaea.

HEBE 6

"I intend to live forever, or die trying"

- Groucho Marx

~*The Voyages of Gaea*~

Gaea had 'turned the corner' in her explorations. Many years had past since her launch, her inhabitants started to feel the pull of home. More and more, the crew members found themselves looking out the portholes, wondering which point of light harbored their families and loved ones. This was an ancient and honored tradition, starting with sailors from long ago plying the waves in their wooden sloops and barks. A sailor during the latter point of a voyage can usually be found leaning on a rail, equally separated from the other sailors, in silence. They think about home, they envision their families and the lives they left behind. They think about how the sea draws them to voyage. Pilots of aircraft have a similar behavior, where they talk about home when flying and talk about flying when home.

Of course the voyage home is always down hill in a sense. Time moves at a slightly quicker pace, as anticipation augments the lives of the crew. This was the case with the *Gaea* crew as they chose a path through another field of stars, which allowed the Earth's sun to generally be centered in the windshield.

One of the worlds they passed was worthy of a closer look. This world was the 6th planet in a Sun like solar system, which the astronomers called Hebe. This, after the

Goddess of youth, dispenser of ambrosia to the Gods, especially Aphrodite. The astronomers thought this world looked young and fresh.

After due consideration, the management staff decided to change course to Hebe 6, go into orbit and possibly send an away team to land on the surface if the environment was conducive.

Once in orbit, the imaging team found land masses, oceans, vegetation and evidence of cities or at least villages. The air was breathable and temperature moderate. The away team was assembled, given instructions and sent on their way. Before departure, the team received word that the inhabitants of Hebe 6 were aware of the visit and had communicated via radio that they looked forward to the meeting. The away team personnel list was adjusted, dropping a geologist in favor of a language specialist. Her name was Angela, conversant in at least ten languages. More importantly, she had a gift of being able to read emotions and intent, even without a complete understanding of a dialect.

The flight from *Gaea* to the surface took a few hours, they landed at an open area outside of a forest, near a village, securing the cabin to prepare for the visit. The door opened to reveal a warm, fresh planet. They stepped

226

out and started walking to the village. Before arriving they met some of the inhabitants, who were to some degree humanoid in appearance.

No two worlds have the same kind of "people." Environments and history conspire to differentiate all beings in the universe, its a well known law. Hebe 6 was no different. The inhabitants were wary but non threatening. Angela was the first to approach one of the villagers. After some brief "discussions" it was obvious that Angela and the villager had an understanding of sorts. The villager pointed towards the direction to his village and then took them to the site. The inhabitants gathered around the visitors

The apparent leader of the village began to speak. The language sounded like Esperanto, an attempt to create a universal language on Earth. Angela listened intently, looking for inflections and meaning. After the initial greeting, the leader raised his hand and smiled.

Angela, sensing one important word in his sentence, raised her hand and said:

"Greetings, we are from Earth, we come in peace.....paco."

"Paco," was the reply.

She pointed to the team members and spoke their names. The leader repeated the names and followed suit

227

naming his companions. What followed was an intensive interchange of words and gestures. Angela and the villagers quickly formed a rapport. The away team members learned several key words and maybe a few phrases within the first several minutes. Angela on the other hand was absorbing most everything that was said and starting to have rudimentary conversations with the villagers. After a particular interchange, she turned towards the away team members and translated.

"They would like us to come to another village to meet the rest of their people. I think they will offer us food and drink as well."

"Sound reasonable," one of the team members said.

The moved as one, following the villagers, over a path lined with trees and bushes, reminiscent of the flora of Earth's Cambrian period. Ancient, simple structures with fern like leaves and simple flowers. The air smelled faintly of sulfur and maybe a hint of salt. As they approached the village, children appeared as well as what turned out to be domesticated pets. These pets were wary of the newcomers and stayed back, staring intently. There seemed to be an absence of elderly versions of the villagers. The crew members noticed this in passing. In fact the vast majority of the people here looked about the same age, mid 30s, interesting.

They moved to the center of the village in an open, public area, with fire pits and benches to sit. Finding places to relax, the crew sat down, while the villagers surrounded them, hopefully out of curiosity. Food and drink did appear as predicted, and slowly the crew members sampled the offerings. The food was mostly fruit like, various colors and tastes. They were all mild, the drink was either water or juice from these fruits. The crew explored their food and ate while the villagers made a fire and gathered closer to try to get to know the visitors.

Soon, there were small, simple conversations going on as the two cultures got to know each other. The language was not too hard to learn, the villagers had the equivalent of verbs and nouns. They pointed to various objects and spoke the names. The crew quickly repeated the words and found acceptance with their efforts. It was learned during the voyage of *Gaea* that it is always best to communicate in the indigenous language. Less stressful to the hosts.

Angela continued to converse with the leader, adapting quickly to the language and starting to speak in longer sentences. After a particularly long interchange, she

229

paused, looking at the leader, then slowly and more quietly asked a few more questions. It seemed like she was making sure she understood something very important that she had just learned.

After another pause, she turned back towards the crew members, most busy eating or attempting small talk with the villagers.

"I think I just learned something incredible about these people," she said.

The away team leader, Jeff, replied: "What? Is it something serious? Something we need to be concerned about?"

"Well, I asked the leader of these people several times about their lifespan. He replied in no uncertain terms that this particular group does not have a lifespan. In fact they have no idea how old they really are. They remember hundreds or maybe thousands of annual cycles, which I think is close to our definition of a year. They remember geological events, and the evolution of their flora and fauna."

"What about the younger ones?"

"Well, this particular group has had thousands of children. They grow like we do and age as we do, until they die. There are many villages around here that have normal

230

life cycles, this one does not."

"Wow, do they attribute their long lives to anything particular?"

"There're not sure. The technology is not advanced enough for them to understand genetics or advanced medicine. From what I understand, they have common colds like we do, break bones and sustain other injuries, but their bodies, unless the injuries are very serious, just heal. This group was much larger in the past but natural disasters and accidents have claimed several of their people."

"That's absolutely amazing," said the away team leader. "Is there any chance they will allow us to do a medical exam of one of their people?"

"I'll ask, but I don't think we should move too quickly, at least until we have obtained their trust."

"That makes sense, ask when you feel its appropriate."

The evening wore on, with the villagers and crew members communicating in more and more efficient ways. Every once in a while, laughter could be heard and many people smiled. At some point it became obvious that the villagers, although comfortable with their new guests, were getting tired. The crew members sensed this and looking toward their leader, began to make plans to leave for the

231

night.

Angela was still talking to village leaders and realizing that a move was about to be made, paused.

After a few seconds, she leaned over to one of the leaders and quietly asked a few questions. Without hesitation, the leader responded and smiled. More words were exchanged, then Angela rose and moved towards the now gathering crew members. Within a few moments, all of the crew was together in a group and in unison started to walk back to the shuttle landing area.

"Did you ask?"

"Yes, they would be happy to help us. In fact, they are very interested in what we might discover. I believe that they feel that in some ways the long lives that they have experienced has been a curse. They have outlived so many loved ones that they are in a way lonely. Also, none of them are married, they tell me that the lack of change in their lives is stressful. They have no life changing experiences to share with a mate. They stay together because of their common attributes, many have tried over the many years to live in another village, but end up feeling very uncomfortable as they outlive everyone and cannot establish meaningful relationships. I don't think they want to die particularly, just move on. So, yes they are very

232

interested in what we can discover.

"That's amazing, you would think that immortality would be the key to discovering the universe."

"They lack the motivation to do so and are very comfortable here. In a way, their minds are full. They have experienced millions of events and because of that, new things become ephemeral."

"So they're done exploring? They're not curious anymore?"

"I think they are pretty much done. One of them amuses himself by watching the stars move amongst themselves. That is a very long drawn out game as you can imagine. That should give you a sense of what they do for fun."

"Wow, okay, well lets take some samples tomorrow, nothing too invasive. We don't want to scare them."

"Oh, that emotion is long gone in these people. All of them have had broken bones and been attacked by wild animals, they just heal and go on."

The team leader moved to the front of the pack and led the rest of the group to the shuttle and then started the preparation for a night's stay. The team talked amongst themselves for the most part that night, making plans and discussing their impressions of the encounter with the

233

"ancient ones." Soon they began to grow tired and seek comfortable places to sleep. Within an hour everyone was pursuing dreams.

The next morning, as their sun rose in the West, so did the crew members. Gathering around breakfast and coffee, they planned their day and started to gather their backpacks and medical supplies to begin testing the locals. A plan was made to test the oldest, the youngest, and the middle aged members of the clan. Blood tests mainly, but with particular attention to history, physical attributes and general health.

They walked to the village area where they had met the evening before. The villagers were waiting, with a curious look in their eyes. They were thinking that the new knowledge of their "affliction" would allow them to experience the final chapters of their lives. To grow old like their ancestors with grace and dignity. Slowly giving their mental faculties to the specters of illusion and repetition. To become themselves, only more so.

Strange it seems that as humans, the crew members, who had not experienced such long life or known anyone who had, would see life as unfortunately short. There is a point in time for all humans, where immortality seems like a very attractive option. Later of course, the

234

chemicals in our bodies conspire to convince us of our Autumn and to move aside to allow the young ones to do the hard work. The "ancient ones" here had been stuck in the working age and had not had the option of being the old masters directing the younger members in the arts of life and creation.

The crew members chose their marks and proceeded to draw blood, make notes of the morphological attributes and interview the subjects regarding their past and family. Soon a few dozen sample kits were complete, ready to be analyzed and compared. Several of the kits were taken immediately to the shuttle for preliminary analysis, just to get a feel for the answer to the riddle.

In a few hours, a medical team member returned from the initial analysis. She bore a curious look on her face and walked directly to the team leader.

"Can we talk?"

"Of course." the leader said, "In private."

"No, that is not necessary, but we should keep it to just a few people for now....certainly until we get a more complete analysis of our findings."

"Fine, lets sit over by that large stand of trees, away from the central part of the meeting area."

They moved to the new spot and sat down.

The team leaded insisted, "Ok, lets hear it."

The medical technician, when she felt that she was not in earshot of the other villagers began speaking in a lowered voice.

"Its rather amazing, our preliminary results show they have the ability to correct abnormalities in their genetic code. As our cells reproduce, minor mistakes occur during the copy phase, after many generations, obvious changes take place, which result in aging. In our case the telomeres, which are the end components of our chromosomes, help to replicate our cells, but sometimes not perfectly. In their case, each time their cells go through the copy phase, the results are perfect. So, as a consequence, they do not age, and all injuries are healed. In fact, it might be possible for them to grow back an organ or a limb if it is injured or removed. Quite remarkable. In fact....."

In complete silence, several of the villagers appeared next to the leader and technician. One spoke.

"Did you discover the secret?"

The technician replied, "The results are preliminary but hold important clues to your 'condition'. "

"We know our condition, we're immortal, and always have been. Have you discovered anything further?"

236

"Not yet, further analysis will give us more information, but we probably have to use our labs onboard the main ship."

"No need."

"No need? I don't understand."

"We're the Nereids."

"I'm sorry," said the leader, "I'm not familiar with that name."

"We are the offspring of the 50 original Nerieds, the daughters of Nerius and Doris the Oceanid, in the history of the Earth's Greek culture. The daughters married the young men of the indigenous inhabitants of this world. We are the offspring and share their traits. Some of us did not live as long because of the sharing of genes. But we, the ones in this village carry the original gifts of the ancient gods of Greece."

The team leader asked, "But the time of the Greek Gods was so long ago, how did your parents find their way to this planet? We thought the Greeks were not capable of traveling through space."

"An advanced culture from a distant solar system, set about to discover the inhabitants of worlds near their own. They built a large ship and spent several generations exploring space. During the voyage, scientists onboard

237

~The Voyages of Gaea~

their ship discovered how to control the reproduction of the cellular structure and as a result the original members of that ship became what you would call immortal. Really nothing more than the progress of science. But compared to many cultures they met during their journey, this was magic. Upon discovering Earth, they decided to introduce themselves to the inhabitants of Greece, as they were the most advanced at that time. The fact that they did not age caused the Greeks to believe they were Gods. They stayed for a few hundred years and as the political climate changed and the impact of their presence became a problem, they left and came to this world."

"An interesting parallel to our journey," observed the team leader, "several cultures we met probably thought *we* were gods."

"Of course. Its common across the cosmos. Cultures are all at different levels, It the nature of living things to be in awe of life at a higher level."

"What will you do here? Here in paradise?"

"Continue to live simply and improve ourselves. We believe that it is written in the starlight and in the lines of our palms that we should live in deeds not years, thoughts not breaths, feelings not measurements from a scientific instrument. We count our time in heart throbs and believe

238

that who lives most is who thinks most, feels the noblest and acts the best."

A long silence ensued after these words, the team from *Gaea* absorbed the phrases along with the perfect evening which had fallen faintly and faintly fallen across the meadows and forests of the land. Without discussion, as the team had descended into a mental harmony, they arose, viewed their superiors and started for the shuttle craft. Every succulent breath was appreciated from that moment on. In silence, the team prepared the craft, each gave one more look out of a window and they lifted off for the mother ship, better than when they arrived.

239

ECHOS OF HOME

"The miracle is not to fly in the air, or to walk on the water, but to walk on the earth."

\- Chinese Proverb

The great ship continued the journey home, still several years away but for once in a very long time, the space farers started to think about what their return would mean. There was of course the anticipation of seeing loved ones that had kept in touch with the crew members, and there was the wonderment of how they would be received once their arrived. More importantly though, the crew members had gone through a metamorphosis, an evolution into a new society. Its important to realize when talking about them, that they, all one thousand or so of them, were now a unique group of beings. They had discovered many new species of humanoids and countless species of flora and fauna. Their catalogs were full and would have a profound effect on the understanding of life in the universe, which was plentiful. Their contributions to the natural sciences rivaled the HMS Beagle and the Lewis and Clark expeditions in the early 1800's on Earth.

Something else though had occurred in the hearts and minds of the crew members. Yes, a profound change in perspective, but also a sense of culture amoungst themselves. They looked at their return to Earth in both a positive way as well as having a sense of forbodding. So many of the crew members had spent most or all of their lives on board the ship that was in all respects, their home and legacy. Most would not feel comfortable leaving the ship for an extended time, as would be the expectation upon their return. The young children in fact, would have significant issues. Looking into the future saw these kids returning to the ship, or at the very least, returning to space in the new, larger ships that would be assembled for the next space voyagers to go forth.

Unlike the merchant mariners of 17th century Earth, where life at sea was both attractive and arduous, the space mariners had found a life so comfortable and rewarding that they much preferred living in that way. Earth, and many other planets, although beautiful in their own ways, lacked the thrill of constant discovery which can most easily be found in space. The observatories on this vessel made almost constant revelations into science and also became very adept in finding other life. During the voyage of *Gaea* in fact, at least 200 more life harboring planets were discovered. This would not have been possible with observatories on atmosphere blanketed planets.

When the crew members had made the mental turn for home, in all of its colors, an interesting event took place in one of the crew assembly halls on the ship. This hall had been converted into a concert venue on many occasions, presenting many forms of music as well as plays, opera and ballet.

Once in fact, a ballet was performed in a reduced gravity setting, the grace and movement of unfettered performers was an unforgettable experience.

On this particular night however, a performance was given by a musician from Earth's Japan. He was a very quiet person in regular life onboard the ship with mundane duties in the food processing plant. Few people who knew him were aware of his training in traditional Japanese music. His talent had been discovered at a very early age and nurtured by constant lessons and hard work with the masters of his land. The journey was not easy, but his gift of interpretation was unequaled. He was discovered by one of the cultural managers of the *Gaea* project before the ship was built and asked if he would be interested in coming along for the journey. He accepted and said he was honored to have the opportunity. Along the way, he found that the pace of work had not allowed him to practice and further his art. Upon the change of course however it was decided to remind the rest of the crew what Earth culture would be like and he was given the time to practice for a concert. He did so in private, as a consequence the organizers of the concert were a bit concerned about what to expect.

243

~The Voyages of Gaea~

He was old now, had only vague memories of life on Earth, but in due course was able with his music to recoup his vision and experiences.

His name was Koichiro Takamizawa, a person enveloped in the culture of his land. Resplendent with a long white beard, a quiet disposition, eyes with a thousand stories in them and a mastery of musical imagery few have had the good fortune to experience. His art was not recordable, as his presence during his performances revealed an aura. An aura that brought the listeners to a foreign land and revealed much more than sound.

On this night, the concert hall filled with a wide variety of people. Many of whom had been alive on Earth and many of whom were born in space. Such a wide chasm of experiences would be a concern to most musicians, it is so difficult to reach an audience from such diverse backgrounds and ages.

Koichiro was unconcerned as he prepared the stage by himself in the dim light of the concert hall. He placed a rug in the center of the stage with a small pillow in the middle. Off to one side a small bamboo plant. Off to the other side a clear vessel of water, near a small pile of rocks. Spartan maybe, but symbolic. It was the tradition of people from the Orient to understand the simple before

244

living with the complex. They had discovered that space and time always exist in the least complex venues.

Several hundred people had now assembled and sat down in anticipation of traditional music. Many of the younger were looking forward to boredom, many of the older were looking forward to sounds that would remind them of their Earth. As it turned our, all would be impressed and moved by forces they did not expect. All would be entranced.

The hall quieted as Koichiro took his instrument, a simple wooden thirteen string zither like apparatus called a Koto. Carved and lacquered, it reflected many of the stage lights onto the audience when moved and set a poly-optical tone. The two meter long instrument made of Paulownia wood was placed on the rug in front of the pillow on which the musician sat, cross legged. His movements to this position were slow, deliberate and graceful. There was a sense that he was not aware of the audience.

Upon finding his balance on the pillow, he looked at the instrument and bowed. A long bow showing his reverence and respect for the ancient machine representing the tones and spirits of the thousands of musicians before him.

He took a long breath, placed his hands on the

245

instrument and played the first chord. A combination of the pentatonic and diatonic scales, the sound created an image of a foreign land. The next chords enhanced the image to reveal a mountain, cool with breeze, near a stream, live with fish. The arpeggios that followed produced the images of snow capped mountains and the airy movement of sound from highs to lows evoked the wind and the pleasing chords that surrounded the voices of the music revealed life in the moving water. The older members of the audience understood the images quickly, the younger were attracted, but for reasons they did not fully understand.

The music moved to another chapter, where a melodic story was being told, the playing of children, romping, carefree, innocent. Koichiro remembered his childhood at this point, the loving face of his mother, the protection of his father, the running and dancing with his brothers and sisters. The sun shone warmly as they played outside, near the trees; games of discovery and revelation where the children would hide behind a tree or bush and dart out laughing. His face while playing twitched a smile.

Next the music moved to sounds of repetition, of scales of patterns of string work that came from his first lessons as a Koto player. The harsh furtive attempts of pleasing sounds from a very difficult instrument. The

246

images revealed the faces of several teaching masters, whose expressions bore the onslaught of a thousand horrible sounds. Work and repetition was heard in the music, until one day the first squeaks resolved into a resonant sound that for a time relaxed the teaching master's face and let him know that patience is a hard profession but boundless in its gifts. The audience approved and agreed with the masters.

The new resonance now blossomed into a melodic tapestry of beauty, as Koichiro remembered his first love. A girl with warm eyes and an unconditional acceptance of his being. Un-complicated was his rapture. It contained the language of wonderment and appreciation as he remembered talking with her about anything and everything. They interpreted life together and walked hand in hand in the forest, inhaling the life abundant. His music at that time was poetic and painted tapestries of adoration. The audience appreciated both the color and inexperience of this chapter.

Next he moved to an image of his education and concentration on his music as his first love, like so many other first loves, was ephemeral. More ardent musical tones were constructed showing his path to refinement. The music became methodical and clear in purpose, almost marching. The trail of hard work seemed obvious as the audience experienced the hard bumps of the musical tones laboring to a conclusion. The listeners were however rewarded with a most pleasant of conclusions as the new musical discoveries rewarded by hard work, emerged to a pleasant, resolved emulation of music with the contributions of previous masters imbedded in it.

Below in the lower decks of the ship, technicians had finally installed new filters that would have the effect of freshening the air and allowing the more pleasant aromas to propagate through the ship. This had taken years of research to perfect, many air samples had been taken of Earth and all of the worlds that had been visited during their voyage. The filters were complex and cumbersome but tonight they were in place and the final electrical attachments had been made. Unbeknownst to the concert goers upstairs, their environment was about the change. The supervisors in the air exchange division decided to introduce the new air slowly and subtly so as not to alarm the crew members, the change was to take place over an hour's period. Valves were turned and switches thrown.

Upstairs in the concert hall, Koichiro continued his artistry. The next harmonies revealed his maturation into an artist. The tone palette took the old masters' work to new

248

levels and in the clearest way showed the audience richer colors and musical ideas that were of the purest art. Emotions started to stir in the listeners as the resonance of ideas to thoughts comforted and caressed the ears of the beholders.   The piano sonatas of Schumann and Chopin were sensed within the room.

Koichiro paused now, brought the emotions back to Earth and regrouped his thoughts.   The next chords and harmonies cleared the palette for his final image, that of Mother Earth. The original sounds of the mountains, water and fish were repeated but with the embellishments of a long life of musical work and its polishing effects. Earth was waiting for the crew members now, as beautiful as it had always been.   In fact, for some reason, the concert goers felt a new freshness in the air, transforming the experience of listening to this wondrous music to a complete sense of a new beginning. Chills ran down many spines.

The final musical notes were both appreciated and missed as their echos finally diminished in the concert hall. Silence took hold for several moments, the older listeners remembering the moving story, the younger listeners impressed by the technique and musical prowess of the Koto player. The lights started to come up and applause was immediate and prolonged. Koishiro rose and bowed for a significant period, then slowly gathered his instrument and props and made his way to the stage exit.

Everyone took in a deep breath of the now fresher air.

The audience had been transformed. The mental courses had been to a degree altered as now many people had long discussions of returning home. The positive attributes of Earth were balanced against a life in space, exploring and discovering. Many guesses were made as to how many people would leave *Gaea* and how many would stay or move to another ship. It felt like a new race had been born, as long as the ship was safe and provided all amenities, "why leave?" Many thought. "Why stay?" Thought many others. It was a difficult period for most, however the journey was not done yet. Many new experiences would be had by all before they saw the blue planet growing larger in the windows.

The hallway emptied with the exception of a few couples who became engaged in conversation.

"That was magnificent, who was he?"

"All I heard was that he was from replen, down in lower level four.

"Wow, reminded me of what the geriatrics say about home."

"Yeah, I've been thinking about that, what are you going to do when we get there?"

"I'm not sure, its a few years away, but I have been thinking about it for a long time. Most of my life has been on this ship, all of my friends, my job, my life's experiences. I really would feel lost without it."

"I know what you mean. I've been thinking about it as well. They say there are new ships being constructed in orbit around Earth. Much larger, with up to ten thousand people on board. Would you consider moving to one of those?"

"Maybe, that sounds so big and impersonal. I'd get lost on one of those things. At least I have seen most of this one and feel comfortable. Do you know what will happen to *Gaea*?"

"Its going to be retrofitted and sent out again. Of course it will go to different star systems, probably for the same length of time."

"I don't know, I feel so comfortable here....did you know that most of the newborns in the hospital section have many differences compared to Earth babies."

"No, I didn't know about that, what differences?"

"They have larger brains and smaller muscles.

251

Most of the parents have been living in a reduced gravity area of the ship and they think that this has effected the babies."

"Interesting. I wonder if that means that they will have trouble on Earth, with higher gravity etc."

"Not only that, but we live in a protected environment, where the air is good, food is good quality of life is good. Harmful bacteria, viruses and microbes are filtered out. I think the doctors are concerned."

"I'll bet. Well let me know what you are going to do. And, oh by the way, we are the last ones in the concert hall."

"Ok lets leave. By the way why do you want to know what I am going to do?"

"Well because I want to go where you go."

They smiled, comfortable with their friendship and in touch with a sense of foreboding upon their return to Earth.

Koichiro Takamizawa gathered his things and after bowing again to a few impressed audience members, moved down the hallway towards his quarters. It had been a long day, and a draining concert. He was happy he had practiced so much before tonight but exhausted by its culmination. He walked slowly and methodically to his room, placed his instrument in its proper place and made some tea. He quarters, although spartan, had a special feature. After he made his tea and basking in his drained state, he walked over to a small table, just one foot off the ground and sitting cross-legged, looked out the window. A window in itself would be special, but this one had the good fortune of facing forward. He looked for Earth.

~The Voyages of Gaea~

TEMPTATION

"Simplicity is the ultimate sophistication"
- Leonardo DaVinci

~The Voyages of Gaea~

A few years remained in their homeward journey, life was routine. On their return path however there were still a few planets that looked like they contained life, to what degree was hard to tell due to the distances that they were first discovered from.

Gaea shifted course by less than a degree to visit the first world, which they named "Gnossos" after the Greek city on Earth, home of Heraclitus, a famous pre-Socratic philosopher who among other things declared "you can never step in to the same river twice." This declaration in essence meant that all things change to some degree, all of the time. So it is impossible to make immutable statements in any endeavor. Science continues to refine its theories, medicine continues to discover new cures and biological mechanisms, philosophy continues to reveal new insights into being.

This new world was a reflection of Heraclitus's ideas as it was a water world with many very large floating islands on it. Most of these islands were several miles deep, made of mostly organic matter with with sprinklings of rocks and dirt collected from the root structures as they passed through shallow seas. These islands were guided through their journeys by well established ocean currents and meteorological phenomenon. They danced around

255

Gnossos over years of time, sometimes brushing up against other islands where flora and fauna could interchange. Some islands became permanently attached to others and with their now greater mass, moved slower and towards the planet's equator. The smaller islands tended to move farther towards the poles and could as a result get colder during the winter seasons.

Life was abundant on these islands, many of which were hundreds if not thousands of miles in size. Trees, plants and higher forms of life had evolved over many millions of years.

The particular solar system Gnossos was a member of had large gas giants to clear away most comets and asteroids, keeping the smaller planets relatively safe. Gnossos also had a moon, albeit denser than Earth's and in a more elliptical orbit. This orbit had the effect of influencing the tides on Gnossos to a significant degree. The islands rose and fell hundreds of feet during the moons voyage around the planet.

Polar caps of ice also existed and island dwellers of the smaller floating biospheres caught glimpses of the ice once every many years.

During the evening, when it was not cloudy, the residents of these islands watched the stars move over the course of the night both from the movement of the whole planet as well as the rotation of the islands. Until a compass like instrument was discovered, this stellar movement was not well understood and was at times the basis of irrational stories predicting the future or the moods of the greater undefined beings said to be constantly observing and evaluating the lives of the inhabitants.

Some of the inhabitants were interesting in that they had green skin, which photosynthesized during the day. The consequences of this was that they drank a lot of water and had root like appendages which constantly sought the ground. They had to be careful where they slept, which was generally in the trees as when they slept too long, especially while lying on the ground, their "roots" would dig deep and make it painful to rise. These roots had to be trimmed periodically but during their version of a wedding ceremony and during mating, the roots took on a life of their own. When these creatures died, they were placed over fertile ground and as their roots (being the last organs to expire) found the ground, the expended bodies became plant food and the roots grew into trees. Years later, as the now mature trees (or bushes and smaller plants in the case of animals and other fauna) pollinated, the cycle became complete when seed pods begat a new sentient being.

Once the crew members discovered this fact, they had a newfound appreciation for the flora of the lands.

These facts and impressions were discovered by the first exploratory missions from *Gaea* as it had altered course to get a closer look at this world. Several teams were dispatched by shuttle to land on several of the more interesting looking islands. The teams found intelligent life on one of the islands in the form of race of bipedal marsupials. These life forms were friendly and without fear and gladly shared the knowledge of their race with the newcomers. They lived harmoniously with their form of nature and found little need to get "technological."

The crew members from the Earth ship found ways to communicate and discovered that the island inhabitants wished them to stay, this as a way to further their culture and understand to a greater degree to unusual wanderings of their stars.

In addition, the weather and climate of this planet was found to be highly variable and apt to change on short notice. Most of Gaea's weather department personnel visited this world and after much soul searching, several elected to stay.

This particular crew had been very busy during the various stops at other planets, but in general very "unbusy"

258

between planets. It was their nature to feel the wind in their faces and tempt fate by getting close to Nature and measuring her vital functions. Many of this crew had chased severe storms and tornados on Earth. Many had taken radars and atmospheric probes into hurricanes and typhoons as well. The thrill of the chase was absent for the most part on this space voyage and they felt empty as a result.

This planet however was alive with weather, as the islands danced across the seas, they changed weather patterns, experienced variations in solar flux and moved from extremes of cold to extremes of warmth. All this was a recipe for significant changes in weather, almost on an hourly basis. The weather folks were inthralled and considering that within a year, they would be back to a well studied Earth and considering also that there was so much to learn about exo-planetary weather, many of the crew decided to make homes on this new planet.

The evening campfires had many interesting conversations during their stay with *Gaea* orbiting above.

From one of the scientific program managers:

"We need to discuss why we should or should not go back to Earth, many of us still have families there or at least remnants after these 40 years in space (75 years in

259

Earth time). My memories are from early childhood, and considering all that I have witnessed during our voyage, I wonder what the big attraction is. Many of the older folks on board and anxious to get back, which is understandable. Many of the young amongst us consider it just another world to explore. They have heard, read and viewed details of Earth, it is after all considered our real home. But I am just not sure how we will react coming home and trying to restart our lives after so many decades."

A younger person to the left of the campfire, now burning quietly:

"There is nothing there for me except relatives I have never met. We are reasonably close and I think that there will be more shuttles and spacecraft coming our way in the future. We have a choice then as well as now in terms of staying."

Another person, this time from the right, who is poking the fire's embers to redistribute the heat:

"My understanding is that Earth is overcrowded now, dark from pollution and controlled by greedy people. Religions zealotry and political ideologies continue to cause wars and destruction. I have absolutely no interest in returning. Look at this place. It's beautiful, it's paradise in every way, with a friendly population. I know for sure that

260

the lower stress from living here will allow us to live longer and happier lives."

A voice from the back of the crowd:

"But how do you know we will not bring those ills with us and introduce them to the local population?"

An answer:

"Because we are a small group, larger groups tend to create subgroups on the basis of common ground, mutual interests, etc. Although larger groups allow for the possibility of more geniuses, more artists, more great scientists, smaller groups co-exist more harmoniously. This is because the smaller group individuals are forced to resolve their problems one way or another. In the case of a larger group, the individuals can always move to another group and find others with similar thought styles."

Silence for a while followed these comments, each individual contemplating where they stood.

"Um, I am going to sleep on this and make a decision tomorrow," one said. And with that most rose to find a place to sleep, a decision had to be made quickly as *Gaea* was soon to depart on the final leg to Earth, or home, depending on how you looked at.

The next day the sun rose in a completely different place than it had the day before, due to the rotation of the

261

10 mile wide island. Soon, someone said, another island was to brush up against the one they were on. Depending on the energy of the collision, the islands might cling together for a while, spinning at a slower rate and if they continued to be connected over a period of weeks or months, the inhabitants would experience less variations in weather and warmer temperatures. No one could predict however, what would happen.

It came to pass that the more individualistic members of the meteorological team decided to stay in an attempt to make a life for themselves. There were 38 of them in total, the managers of *Gaea* understood their decision, outfitted them with communications equipment, food, shelter materials and bid them farewell. The pioneers watched the evening sky as the large spaceship glowed with increased rocket thruster activity and slowly faded into the constellations.

"My god, what have we done?"

"We did what others have done, the European explorers, the pioneers in America, the first Moon colony.....its in our blood. Oh and by the way, we are gods now."

Several smiled at this thought.

Months later, the colony was still in place, having

weathered storms both inside and out of their confines. They rediscovered their human spirits and even with the challenges of creating a stable life in terms of food and shelter, they managed to be successful.

Their communications gear chattered periodically, asking for updates. The members of the "Weather Colony" would interact with the mother ships personnel but after a while, it seemed less attractive to do so. Many times the radio would come alive and many of these times the colony members would just watch the displays and status lights of the equipment and not answer.

They were simply content.

A HEROS' JOURNEY

"Throughout the Universe, the story is the same: the laws of physics are the laws of physics, the laws of life are the laws of life; you put the same ingredients in the pan, heat it up, and you will have a cake."

- Carl Sagan

The captain leaned back in his chair squinting, just able to discern the blue dot which is Earth.

A voice from behind, "How do you feel about coming home?"

"I don't know. However it doesn't matter, my job is to follow the orders of the 14 captains that came before me. I swore an oath to complete the mission."

"You and Neil Armstrong....and Paul Tibbets."

"Maybe," he looked back at his navigator, "I will complete the mission as I said, after that who knows. We come back as a group of people with a completely new perspective on life in the universe. I don't even know if we will fit into our society when we return. Frankly I think there will be problems acclimating and," he turned back to face the pale blue dot in the window, "I would not be surprised if many of us come back to this or another exploratory ship to go back out again."

"I think you're right, as do most of the crew members. Its quiet in there these days," the navigator pointed to the spinning crew's quarters and living spaces. "We learned so much and as a consequence became a different society compared to the one we left."

"How long do we have?" queried the Captain.

"Just over a month." was the reply.

"Are arrival preparations in full swing?"

"Think so, I know that most items have been checked off the list. Many to go but my guess is that we will still have some action items open. Nothing safety related of course, mainly because Earth is just another stopping place like the rest. The difference will be navigating around the incredible amount of space hardware that is in orbit. We are probably going to be hit a few times by debris."

"Ok then, lets consider a very high orbit initially, we will scan for the orbiting debris first and then make a decision on going lower. If we have to start from a geo-stationary orbit to keep out of harm's way, let's do it."

"Roger that."

"Is radar picking up anything?"

"A few things, several interplanetary probes, some junk of some sort. No problem for us to navigate around for now. I have already programed the flight management computer."

"Okay, good. We will start the the pre-landing checklists at the usual times, then."

"Roger that."

"Okay, I am going to meet with the CEO for the next hour, call me if you need anything."

"Shall do, Captain."

With that, the Captain rose from his chair and "walked" to the rear of the cockpit room. Waiting his turn in the rotating hallway he stepped onto the moving stairway and started the decent into gravity and the office areas. He had done this many times before, but this felt different. Like the culmination of a very long journey with only weeks left, he had a mixture of emotions.

The crew of *Gaea* had been observing Earth for a long time, in fact they had discerned the seasons and examined the atmosphere. The reports started coming in at least a year before they were to enter orbit. On the night side of Earth, the many lights of civilization could be seen, on the day side, the blue oceans beckoned. With the solar wind, it seemed like the blue marble twinkled a bit. Most on board viewed the forward camera monitor channel being broadcast by the servers. Again, to many, it was just another world to explore.

Four fifths of the crew had never seen Earth, they had been told, educated and convinced that it was a wonderful place. But the new space perspective curbed the enthusiasm for a return, or more accurately, an end to the journey. An informal poll of the crew found that most would not mind spending their lives onboard the ship discovering new worlds. It was Earth inverted, instead of standing on, it

267

was standing in. Same but different.

Communications were increasing in bandwidth as they approached. Full access to the Earth's Internet was available, with crew members contacting long lost relatives. Many were contacting relatives of relative, once or twice removed due to the intervening 75 years. Although interested, the twice removed relatives felt little connection with the space farers. In a way that was okay. The big concern of course is what Earth had become over the long period.

The new "*Gaen*" society had gotten used to significant differences relative to Earth society. Many of these differences were predicted by Science Fiction writers many years ago. The first difference was the lack of money usage. There simply was no point for it on a space ship. Accumulation of wealth was an archaic obsession, where the accumulator felt in some way superior to the others, as in a special skill or gift. Gifts and skills were present on *Gaea* and appreciated for what they were, having the most acorns or candy wrappers did not mean much.

Economic transactions on Earth were now done solely with the Internet, the added convenience also opened the door to massive Internet crime. If one was lucky, massive encryption would keep most of the financial

268

transactions safe. But just the statistical amount of data transfer gave the thieves information about who was doing a lot of what. The infrastructure was so Internet based that disruptions in service could be catastrophic. Ransom on the cutting of fiber optics cables became commonplace.

Also, technology with regards to individuals had become very sophisticated. Once a long time ago, someone had asked "Would you give up privacy for safety?" This was done right after a terrorist attack when the public was anxious and afraid of what the future held. They answered "absolutely!" and thus began the massive public monitoring policies, which grew more powerful than the progenitors had ever imagined. Everything was monitored, all human activity, including interaction, communications, movements, attitudes and propensities. An individual with unique political ideas was flagged and numerically evaluated as a danger to society. When the numbers got too high, even without a crime committed, the person would be contacted and educated as to the length and breadth of the government's interest in their activities. Face recognition, voice recognition and a host of other electronic tagging means traced the activities of everyone from birth to death. For the huge server farms, it was easy. On the surface, walking into a store and buying something was

269

stress free. A person would make a selection and walk out of the store, the electronics would take care of the transaction by just recognizing the individual and their item of choice. If you did not have the money for the purchase, alarms would sound and someone or something would come and get you. Genetic profiling at birth dictated what health care you would be provided during your life, sans any accidents. Proper food and exercise was mandated by the insurance industry, in order to maintain your health care coverage. Certain activities became illegal based on risk, like mountain climbing and parachuting.

To assimilate the crew into such a controlled environment caused concern, even to the point of the creation of a movement to visit, drop off any people who wanted to stay, pick up any supplies and immediately fly off in a new direction.

Looking at the Captain, "We gotta problem, chief."

"Yeah, I know. People are not thinking things out, they're getting emotional and if we don't do something, things will get out of hand.

"Yep, they have voted to keep going and have chosen representatives to address the Board."

"Ok, I guess we will have to deal with that. I think though that it will be important to address everyone over the

270

intercom before they get serious. Let everyone know that I will address them tonight at 1900 local."

"Okay Captain, I will let them know."

1900 was only a few hours away, the Captain sat with members of the board for a while, then retired to his quarters to think. Some of the points were valid, but people were exaggerating the issues based on what they were hearing and seeing from Earth. The media was part of the problem as it had the tendency to focus on the more sensational issues and not the mundane. What was getting lost was the details of the everyday lives of the people living on Earth, which for the most part was reasonable, happy and content.

The ship was now a few weeks away from orbit, the thrusters had slowed the ship to a mere 25,000 miles per hour. Now the image of Earth was getting larger in the view screens and the windows. The crew members could see faint lights on the night side, clouds on the day side. The internet channels were full of data transfer and family interactions. Telemetry from the voyage was singing down the microwave channels, crowding the frequency space and running the downlink computers at full speed with video and other high speed traffic. The crew members looked out of the windows, some packed, some refused to pack and

271

some sat in their quarters and worried.

At 1900 the Captain came on the intercom as advertised.

"This is the Captain. We are now 520 hours from orbital insertion. The mission has been a resounding success as we have made history, all of us. The people of Earth are anxious to meet us and have prepared celebrations, parties and special events for any of us who want to participate. I encourage all of you to consider doing so as we all deserve to be thanked for our sacrifice, courage and dedication. The amount of data during our mission of discovery is so vast that the downlink computers will need months to transfer it. It will take years to be thoroughly understood and decades to fully appreciate. Each one of us has participated in discoveries that will leave us individually changed forever but more importantly, humanity will reap the bounties of our findings for thousands of years. We discovered life in so many places, we can declare that life is abundant in the Universe. This is a giant leap for mankind as well as a small step for those in this ship. Neil Armstrong would be proud of those words had he known that we invoked his spirit of exploration once again. I know however that many of you are concerned about what we will find on Earth, now that it has been 75

272

years since this ship left orbit, left families and left connections to our once home. Things are different now and I would be less than honest if I told you that I was not concerned about these differences. But we have to think about history, our history which is down there on the surface of that blue planet we see out of the windows. We have to think about the people, *our* people, who are waiting for us. And we have to think about ourselves, who are made of the substance and souls of those we left. They are us, and we are them. It would be irresponsible for both sides to see the other as something different. We have heard stories about life on Earth, much different that what we left. We on this ship hold perspectives that will enlighten and warm the lives of those below, it would be selfish of us not to share those perspectives."

On Earth, the amateur astronomers had found the ship and began giving updates on its position using the internet. The professional astronomers had located the ship long ago and had moved onto more pressing research

The ship entered orbit and crew transfers started to take place. At first, small groups came down to Earth, mostly the upper management from the ship, who came down to meet the upper management of the space agencies and governmental entities. Some speeches were

273

made, some fanfare, but most curiously, there was a lack of detailed de-briefings.   It was expected by the crew members of *Gaea* that there would be many months of report writing and interviews. This did not happen. In fact, there was a general lack of interested in the return, mostly obligatory interactions were observed.   Many crew members who transported down from the ship were greeted politely and allowed to just move on. This was not by any means expected and colored the reactions of the crew members as to whether or not they should visit the Earth. As a result, the transportations slowed, some crew members actually went back up on return shuttle flights.

Many did stay on Earth however, they had been in the wilderness long enough and sought a comfortable life on the planet.   They became the story tellers and chroniclers of the great voyage. What they found on "the ground" was a population concerned about their own plight. They were dealing with economics, pollution and basic needs. The crew members from the ship taught them how to conserve, live efficiently and be self sufficient.

It was the natural order of things.

EPILOGUE

One Spring morning, there was a knock at the door. Judee Dublin stood at the entrance, anxious about what reaction the family inside would have with her arrival.

The door opened, "Yes, may I help you?"

"Um,   I am Judee Dublin, daughter of Mamie Dublin, sister of Nancy."

"I am Nancy, how are you Judee?" This with a tearful reaction as the door we opened further and Judee entered. The sisters, twins in fact, had seen pictures of

275

each other over the years during the voyage. But the compression of time had changed Judee little and changed Nancy much. In fact there was a 35 year difference between them, even though they had been borne seven minutes apart.

"Hello, Aunt Judee," came a voice from within the house. It was Emily, who was now about the same age as her aunt. Judee looked around the home, noticed the pictures, warm tones of colors from the walls and the views out the windows. It was Fall now on Earth, there had been no seasons on Gaea, no movement of the Sun, no moon. The smells were usually the same, not like having a kitchen, flowers, spices and grass. The sounds were foreign as well; traffic, wind, dogs. Judee took a deep breath, found a place to sit and asked for a cup of Tea.

"That must have been an amazing experience," said Emily, "do you have any stories from your journey?"

GLOSSARY

EVA – Extra Vehicular Activity, in space when an astronaut leaves the confines of the capsule, shuttle or space station.

Fast Pants – G suit worn by fighter pilots and aerobatic pilots to keep blood from pooling in the legs during high G turn.

Scintillation – Changing air density causes stars to twinkle or scintillate. This phenomenon is also prevalent in radio wave propagation. While listening to short wave stations for instance, the volume of the signal rises and falls as the intervening medium changes transmission characteristics.

ABOUT THE AUTHOR

"Writing books allows me to learn about things"

Kevin Shoemaker was born in New York City in April of 1954. A son of an actress and musician turned professor. He has lived in several states and has been educated in the fields of philosophy, radio astronomy and antenna design. He has authored several technical papers and has nine patents in the fields of aviation, antenna design and meteorology. In addition, he is an avid pilot and boat owner and holds several certificates for operating aircraft, helicopters and performing flight instruction. Currently he works as an antenna and radar designer in Colorado. Mr. Shoemaker is a father of one daughter and one son and lives near Boulder with his wife, Judi.

Comments?   e-mail: Thevoyagesofgaea@gmail.com

Other books by the author:

Mars Life

Practical Antenna Design

www.ingramcontent.com/pod-product-compliance
Lightning Source LLC
Chambersburg PA
CBHW031101260626
47172CB00001B/169